The Appeal of Stalking

by

Stan Talbott

First published by Dog Ear Publishing
4010 W. 86th Street, Ste H
Indianapolis, IN 46268
www.dogearpublishing.net

ISBN: 978-145750-636-9

This book is printed on acid-free paper.

Any representation of actual living (or non-living) people and/or actual names in the following story is purely coincidental. It is the sole work and opinion(s) of the author. Many of the areas described—Sydney's Harbour Bridge, Portland's Rose Garden Arena, the Oregon Shakespeare Festival in Ashland, and other locations—exist, and were experienced in 2009-2011, yet it is important to stress that this story is a fiction and that the portraits of the characters which appear in it are fictional, as are some of the events and journeys. The author thanks all of the Facebook Hotties for their insight, inspiration, and support, as well as attorneys Jeni Feinberg and Jesse Barton for their perspective, guidance, wisdom, and advice. Thanks also to editor Jim Whiting.

Printed in the United States of America

The following story is dedicated to all parents and children worldwide, who possess a willingness to sit across from each other and talk honestly through their differences, even if this means asking and answering tough questions. In my book, those who can do this are all heroes.

"If you want to be a writer, you have to write every day. You don't go to a well once but daily. You don't skip a child's breakfast or forget to wake up in the morning."
~ Walter Mosley

"There are three things you can do to wayward children. You can love them, suffer for them or you can turn them into literature."
~ Stan Talbott

Prologue

After spending three memorable weeks Down Under, I was looking forward to returning to the States. The cab driver picked me up just after six a.m. I had figured that I'd beat the Friday morning rush hour traffic, and then have breakfast at Sydney's Kingsford Smith International Airport before catching my late morning scheduled Delta flight to Los Angeles. From the back seat of the cab, I could see the iconic Sydney Opera House in the distance across the water as we approached the city's other icon, the Harbour Bridge. Red lights lit up on many of the cars as traffic came to a standstill.

Having given myself plenty of time, I did not think there was cause for alarm. Setting all racial profiling aside, the driver appeared to be from the Middle East, with dark hair, dark beard, dark skin and dark eyes. He seemed relaxed as the meter continued to increase the fare's amount. After about ten minutes of being stuck, I decided to query him.

"Any idea what the holdup is, mate?"

"No, no idea whatsoever," he replied.

"Maybe we could turn the radio on and find out?"

"No worries," he said, as he reached over and turned the dials.

As the volume began increasing, I leaned forward to listen...

"Checking Radio Triple-M traffic for the Sydney area, we now have on the line with us Mac Wolfe, who has currently positioned himself atop Sydney's Harbour Bridge. Mac, what are you doing up there?"

"I've told the authorities. No one will get hurt if they do what I say. I've told them to shut the bridge down. It's mine for the morning."

"So, are you staging a protest? What seems to be the problem here?"

"I'm here for kids that come from broken families. There's no help for them. There's a reason why the government is spending so much on mental health because we aren't letting fathers see their kids. We're letting the kids down."

"Mac, I'm seeing on the television monitors that you've placed two banners atop the bridge. One says, 'PLEASE HELP MY KIDS' and the second says, 'KIDS FIRST'."

"I'm here on behalf of my three children and ALL children who are not being allowed to see their fathers. During the last three weeks I've made ten calls to DOCS, the Department of Child Services, and I have not received one returned call."

"Mac you're making three million people late for work, school, appointments, plane flights and other travel plans."

"And I owe an apology to all of them, but in the grand scheme of things this isn't only about fathers' rights. This is about human rights. We are letting the kids down and we're just throwing good money after bad to failed governmental programs, and I think that's worth everyone taking a bit of time to stop and think about this. It's worth the short delay."

"I hear you, Mac."

"Every kid deserves the right to a loving mother *and* a loving father, and neither parent has the right to alienate their kids from the other parent. I haven't been allowed to see my kids for seventy days, because their mother claims I've been stalking her."

"You know that there's a chance this protest could hurt your cause."

"I'm aware of that, but I'm willing to make necessary changes in my life, and this will help me see my kids sooner. If not, I will be patient and at least my kids will know now that I love them more than ever. The authorities are calling on the other line. I need to go now. Thank you."

"That was Mac Wolfe atop…"

The driver turned down the radio volume and looked at me.

"Well, we now know why we're being delayed."

"Hey look! Is the bloke abseiling from the top of the bridge?" I asked.

"He is!" replied the driver. "He must think he's Spider-man or Batman or Robin!"

Moments later, after he had lowered himself from the top of the bridge, Mac Wolfe had landed on the base of the bridge. Sydney Police immediately swarmed him, and he was arrested.

"So what's your name?" I asked the driver. "I'm Billy."

"I'm Fareed."

"My last name is Freeman. Pleased to meet you, Freed."

"No… it's FUHreed."

"Fuhreed. I gotcha, Fareed. Sorry about that."

"No worries."

"How long have you been in Sydney?"

"Just a few years."

"Where are you from?"

"Pakistan. I've got Australian citizenship after getting married here, but I think I'm about to go through a divorce."

"Yikes. Do you have any kids?"

"Yes, two. My solicitor told me that in Australia you're better off not getting a divorce unless you're going to get remarried immediately."

"Faheed, what's a solicitor? Is that like your marriage counselor?"

"No," he laughed. "You blokes call them *attorneys* in the States."

"Gotcha, Fareed. So why did your solicitor tell you not to get divorced until you're ready to remarry?"

"If men go to court for a divorce and custody issues, they are setting themselves up for two years of pure hell. They don't get to see their kids. The fathers' parents, the grandparents on the dads' side, don't even get to see the grandkids, either."

"What if the mother is psycho, with severe mental issues?"

"There are some exceptions but they have to be extreme cases. My solicitor said he represented a man whose soon to be ex-wife said that she didn't want her kids at the father's home because there were 'entities' inside the father's house."

"Entities? Wow. So what happened?"

"The father's solicitor argued that the 'entities' were in the mother's mind, but the judge ruled that the kids would be better off with the mother until the divorce process was completed and that's what takes two years."

The traffic finally started to move. Fareed turned the radio back on and we listened to the morning's replays and updated reports. We also heard that after his arrest, Mac Wolfe had been rushed to a local Sydney jail, charged and booked for obstructing traffic, climbing on bridges, and jumping off of bridges.

So much for breakfast, I thought when we had finally reached the airport. I was happy, however, that I still had two hours to clear customs and security. I had been Down Under to compete in the Australian Ironman Triathlon competition so I had packed my triathlon bike and all of my gear. I'd also coached at some youth basketball clinics so I had a large amount of luggage.

After making it to the gate, and boarding the plane, I took my window seat and decided to spend the first five hours of the thirteen-hour flight reading a story I'd picked up at the University of Melbourne Book Shop. It was a novel by Aussie author Markus Zusak, titled: *The Book Thief.* After finishing the international best seller, I had eight hours remaining before landing at LAX.

I put on my noise-reduction headphones, turned on permanent repeat in iTunes and selected the Foo Fighters song "Still." I pulled out a prescription bottle from my pocket.

As the plane shook amidst a moment of turbulence, I paused...

I looked down at the bottle, shook my head and smiled as I read the prescription label:

Ambien.

I popped two pills and in an effort to wage the war against jet lag, I drifted off to dreamland. Eight hours later, we landed in Los Angeles at eight a.m., exactly two hours before we had left Sydney. Back to the future, I thought.

After I thought I had smoothly cleared customs, I was held up by a U.S. Immigration and Customs Enforcement official who, according to his badge, was named Officer Hernandez.

"I see there's a restraining order in effect against you, Mr. Freeman," said Hernandez.

"I'm sorry to hear that," I replied. "My attorney was supposed to have had that dropped before I left."

"It's still showing in our system. The person who has the restraining order issued against you is a Diane Downer."

"Yeah. Goddamn her. She's my ex-wife and I honestly thought she was done negatively impacting my life."

Time was ticking away and I sensed a few beads of sweat forming on my brow. I felt stressed a little as to whether or not I would make my connecting flight to Portland. Though I was feeling a bit nervous for being detained, I was curious about something.

"Tell me, Officer Hernandez. I'm wondering why the system didn't stop me when I was here leaving for Australia three weeks ago."

"We aren't concerned about your leaving the country. We're just concerned about your coming into the country."

"Wow, that's interesting."

"Mr. Freeman, are you traveling alone?"

"I am."

"We need to make sure you're not traveling with the person who has the restraining order against you. Unless of course you have court documents stating that it's been approved by a judge for you to travel with her."

"Officer Hernandez, she'd be the last person on Earth that I'd be traveling with."

Forty-five minutes later, Officer Hernandez finally told me I was free to go. As many people already know, navigating LAX can be a pain in the ass. I started really sweating things out. I had to pull my triathlon bike and bags out of the international flights baggage area and then recheck everything for the domestic flight to PDX. Next was jumping the shuttle bus to Terminal 3, which had a massive line waiting for me to clear security for the second time on this trip. I hustled to the gate for the flight to Portland with just seconds to spare.

After finding my seat, and taking off for Portland, I began pondering the journey Down Under. Completing the Australian Ironman Triathlon had to be the most satisfying endurance event of my life. The barrage of obstacles that were thrown my way during the training were unlike any other I'd ever experienced. The problems which posed themselves before me began in Portland, Oregon's largest city where I was calling "Home," twenty-one months earlier. It was September 2009…

CHAPTER 1:

CLEARly Stalking

"Dad, I don't think it's a good idea for you to stop by the store," said my 22-year-old son, Tyler, via cell phone. "Mom is there."

"Son, you don't think it's a good idea for me to stop by any more than I think it's a good idea that you hired your mother. Tyler, this arrangement is blowing up in your face. You don't need to rescue your mother. She was doing just fine working as an EMT in Ashland."

"Dad, you know she wanted to get out of Southern Oregon and besides, I can use her help."

"When I took you and your girl, Holly, out to dinner last month, how much money did you tell me you were going to make off your website sales alone?"

"Dad, I don't want to discuss this."

"Ty, you told me *935,000 dollars a year* for the next two years. What happened?"

"You already know. I told you a week later headquarters said I couldn't keep Google marketing as my creative sales strategy with the *personal* website."

"Exactly, and now I'm going to be straight and blunt with you, Son. When it comes to business, your mom is cursed. She fucked with three of my businesses and she fucked with two of her second husband's businesses. It's only a matter of time before she finds the third husband and he takes the

1

hammer. And it's no wonder that your $1.87 million got flushed down the toilet a week after you hired her."

"When my marketing strategy was nixed, it wasn't her fault. It was going to happen anyway."

"Yeah, Son, but you thought it would be two years down the road."

"I've got sales appointments all over southwest Portland today. I'll be back in by three. Could you stop by then, instead?"

"I probably could, Son, but I'm slammed busy myself. I'm going to be in the area and I need to drop off the extra mobile Internet modem you sold me."

"Isn't there someone you know who can use it?"

"Listen, I bought it because you needed one extra sale two months ago to get a bonus. You're the one who said I could return it. I don't need two modems."

"Could you try not to get in a confrontation with my mom?"

"Sure, Son, I'll give it my best. There are a few things I'd like to discuss with her about your sisters, but I'll try to keep it brief."

"Dad, have you *ever* been able to keep things brief?"

"Good point. There's always a first time. I gotta run."

"Peace, Dad. Please, no fighting with her."

I drove to Tyler's CLEAR store on the 2700 block of North Lombard in Portland. With CLEAR releasing its mobile Internet 4G product, my son got in on the ground level just a few months ago. Even though the economy has been tough, customers have been buying this recession-proof product as if there was no tomorrow.

I opened the door and noticed no customers, but a familiar face behind the counter. It was Diane, my ex-wife. She was on the phone.

"Yes, CLEAR has service in your area. It's only $29.95 per month. Would you like to schedule an appointment to enroll you for service in your home, or in our store?"

Shortly thereafter she finished the phone call. A potential customer had entered and picked up some literature off the counter.

"Sir, are you interested in joining the CLEAR Family today?" asked Diane.

"I'm heading into work but I just wanted to pop in and get an info sheet," he replied. "I'll be back later this afternoon. Gotta run."

"Thanks for coming in," she said as the man exited the store. Her pleasant demeanor immediately halted as she turned her attention toward me.

"Why are you here?"

"Shouldn't I be asking you that same question?" I replied. "I thought you went to school to be a paramedic."

"It was an EMT program. I came up here to help Tyler. I plan to leave after he's up and running, but that's none of your business. Look, I'm about to go to the gym to work out."

"So you've started working out? Congrats. Did you ever stop smoking?"

"You don't have to worry about that either."

"Why not? We have a grandson now and another on the way. It's never been easy shaking loose of your poor judgment, the bad habits and bad examples you set, and the kids have slipped into following your footsteps. Now I have to worry about the damage being done on the new generation."

"Whether I smoke or not is of no concern to you."

"How many people do you know who work out and still smoke cigarettes?"

"I don't want to talk about this subject anymore."

"Do you expect the kids to carry around your oxygen tanks, someday?"

"Can we change the subject?"

"No prob. I talked to Tyler. He said you'd be here. I'd like to return this modem. It's never been used."

"Thanks, just leave it on the counter. Oh, I guess there is something I did want to ask you."

"What is that?"

"How was your brother's wedding, last summer?"

"Tim and Brooke's? It was awesome. I've never been to a wedding in the Redwoods. Simply incredible. Great atmosphere. Good food, music and dancing thereafter... and most importantly... it was all about family. I'm sorry Tyler and Libby chose not to attend."

"I didn't keep them from going. It was their decision."

"Did you encourage them to go?"

"I did. You know Tim invited all three of us."

"I knew that. So why didn't *you* go?"

"I was just super busy with finishing EMT school. I had finals that week. Then I went to Africa after that."

"Africa? That's right. You were saving something to do with the planet. Was it rain forests or gorillas?"

"I visited a number of orphanages, if you must know. So many of the people there are dying of AIDS and their children need help."

"Wow, that's very admirable," I said, facetiously.

"In addition to the orphanages I got to visit a number of African tribes. I even sat in on tribal group therapy sessions. During these sessions, families would sit at a table and meet with the leaders of the tribes to work out their problems. A lot of times I couldn't follow the language or the communication but I could sense they wanted to work out their differences in peaceful and collaborative manners."

"*Collaborative?* Damn, that's good vocabulary."

"Thank you, but I sense you're being sarcastic, again."

"Listen, please don't be offended, but I'm puzzled and curious. Why have you been able to help foreign kids without parents? You have been able to see foreign families firsthand resolve issues, yet you're unwilling to help your *own* kids work out differences with their family members?"

"I don't appreciate the demeaning tone in your voice."

"Sorry about that, Di. Hey, I don't mean to change the subject, but isn't it amazing what our son has been able to accomplish when he's been allowed to be free and creative?"

"I know. I'm so proud of him. And to be honest with you, I've always said that he's gotten his entrepreneurial spirit from you."

"No kidding? You really say that."

"Sure. You've passed on all your sales and marketing skills to him with your competitive fire!"

"Wow! That might be the nicest thing I've ever heard you say."

"You're welcome. You and I both know it's the truth."

"Hey Di, now that you're in Portland are you going to get involved in orphanages in this area?"

"Perhaps. Did you know that Portland has the third highest per capita child trafficking percentage in America?"

"I did not."

"Well, it's a major issue and someone has to help the kids."

"So what's been going on with husband number two?"

"Ryan? Well honestly, he was very supportive. After he paid my way through alcohol rehab and EMT school, he also paid my way to go to Africa. It cost about $5,000 for the month. He probably would have been okay with it but when I got back, I also had a $2,000 cell phone bill because of my daily calls back to Libby."

"Yikes!"

"Yeah, that sort of pushed him over the edge and now we're no longer married."

"Thanks for clarifying. I heard you had gotten divorced, but I wasn't sure why."

"I hate to admit it, but going to African orphanages probably cost me my second marriage."

"Anyway, I do wish Tyler, Libby and even you could have made it to Tim's wedding. You know, there are people in this world who get divorced and then somehow get along with their exes after they go their separate ways. They can even go to family functions and also have conversations without getting angry or being afraid…Sort of like what we're doing now."

"I know that. Jeez, we've been divorced since 2000. Almost ten years now."

"Diane, it was 2001, so almost nine years."

"2000, 2001, nine or ten years, what difference does it make? It's been a long time."

"So are you afraid of me?"

"Are you kidding me?" she laughed.

"Good. Just checking. Just want to make sure you don't think I'm stalking you or anything absurd like that."

"*Stalking?* That is absurd," she laughed.

"Hey, I was wondering something. Now that Libby is working here and her first child will be born in a few months, do you think the three of us could sit down and talk? Maybe work through some issues?"

"She's twenty-six years old. She's an adult, and I can't make her do anything she doesn't want to do."

"Di, look…twenty years ago, back to some of her first memories, she wasn't an adult. Are you absolutely sure you weren't pouring shit into her head when she was little?"

"I'm not going to listen to this."

"I'm not surprised but at least hear me out on this. I've tried everything…cards, gifts, money, phone calls, letters. I just want to know what her issues have been all of these years. Why don't you think daughters need to have a relationship with their dad?"

"That's not what I think."

"Oh, that's right. How are both of your dads doing?"

"You know since I was adopted, I only met Clyde once, back in the nineties. Henry, my adoption dad, isn't doing very well if you must know."

"Are they both still smoking? Probably both hooked up to oxygen tanks by now. They sure taught you well."

"Like I said. I have to get to the gym."

"Okay, who's going to be here when you leave? Do you just shut down?"

"No, somebody's on the way."

"Is it Libby? Maybe we could talk for a few minutes when she gets here, in between customers?"

"She doesn't want to talk to you."

"Look Diane, I've been struggling in my relationship with Libby and you've been having problems with Faith. What if we could do a daughter swap; sit down and have some coffee?"

"I'm not having problems with Faith."

"When's the last time you talked to her?"

"About a month ago."

"Wasn't that the time she had to take her son back from you?"

"Trystan was visiting me in Portland."

"That's not my understanding. You had kept him a week longer than you and Faith had agreed."

"Look Billy, we don't have to go into this either, but everybody knows that he would be better off if I raise him. Faith has a lot of problems."

"Who's everybody?"

"Ty, Libby, and me for starters. Shall I continue?"

"That's why you, Faith, and I should talk. She and I have had a number of conversations and she's even told me some alarming stories about when she was younger."

"Like what?"

"I'd rather let her speak for herself, but since you and I aren't able to find time or the opportunity for all the family members to talk, I guess now is as good as any."

"What?"

"You probably should be surprised by what I'm about to tell you."

"WHAT?"

"I make it a point never to make judgments without hearing both sides of a story. But I'll admit that I'm a little disturbed by some of the things our daughter has started to bring to light."

"Just spit it out."

"Okay, there are questions. First, Faith says that when you were working at the medical offices in Ashland, not only did you routinely take sample anti-depressants and sleeping pills home, but you also used to grind up Ambien and put it in my ice cream so I would go to sleep and we wouldn't fight at night."

"Why would she say a thing like that?"

"Faith says that you didn't want me to bother you since you wanted to smoke, drink a six-pack, read your romance novels, and write in your journals on the back porch. Same routine you had for years. Di, be straight with me…did you put sleeping bills and anti-depressants in my food?"

"I don't want to discuss this."

"Come on, Di! Why not?"

"I'm trying to work."

"I thought you were going to the gym?"

"I am, just as soon as the other person gets here."

Another customer, this time a young girl, entered the store and discussed servicing plans with Diane. I took a seat and waited as Diane enrolled the girl in a CLEAR service plan. When the girl exited, I resumed the conversation.

"Okay, Diane. If you don't want to talk about your putting Ambien in my ice cream, how 'bout this one: Faith says when she was between the ages of eleven to fourteen, you repeatedly crawled into bed with her at night while you were naked, reeking of smoke and alcohol, and she had to slam herself up against the wall away from you in order to get any sleep."

"WHAT?"

"She said that was on the nights you made it to bed. Many times she had to drag your sorry ass in from out of the cold, or you would pass out in the bathroom after shitting yourself."

"I think you need to leave now."

"Di, I hope you aren't still doing this kind of stuff."

"You know I've been sober for almost four years…ever since I went to that rehab program in Boise in 2005."

"I hope you've stayed sober, too. Look, I'm not trying to judge you here or be the jury and convict you. If the other kids were saying things like this to you about me, I would hope you could be a mature parent and bring this stuff to my attention."

"Thank you, but I really think you should go now."

"Okay, I do need to go…but there is one final thing you should know."

"What's that?"

"Did you hit on, and have an affair with, the Ashland High School quarterback?"

"No!"

"Are you sure? Faith told me otherwise. She said it started when the kid was fifteen."

"Who's she talking about?"

"Bobby Robbins, the kid who led the Ashland High Grizzlies to the state championship."

"Leave!"

"Okay, okay, Diane, but you know it wouldn't have been the first time. If what Faith is saying is true, you have committed at least three felonies and you're lucky you've never been thrown in the slammer and that you aren't there right now, for that matter!"

"IF YOU DON'T LEAVE RIGHT NOW, I'M CALLING 9-1-1!"

"Did you sleep with the high school quarterback?"

"I'M CALLING THE COPS!"

The next day, I wasn't actually surprised when a Multnomah County Sheriff's deputy appeared at my office at Wachovia Securities on the tenth floor of the Lincoln Tower in Beaverton, where I worked as a financial advisor.

"Are you Mr. William Blake Freeman?" he asked.

"Yes."

"I'm Deputy Bob Smith. I'm here to serve you with a temporary restraining order."

"From my ex-wife?"

"I believe so. The petitioner is *Diane Christine Downer.*"

"Oh, so she's gone back to her maiden name?"

"I'm not sure, Mr. Freeman."

"She changes her name about every other month so I'm just trying to keep up."

"Okay, Mr. Freeman. I need to serve you this properly. It has been alleged that you have alarmed or coerced the petitioner. If you engage in additional contact that alarms or coerces the petitioner, you may be arrested for the crime of stalking."

"Stalking, are you kidding me, Officer Smith? Surely you aren't serious?"

"Totally serious, Mr. Freeman. I must advise you that you are no longer welcome to contact Diane Downer. You are no longer to make her phone ring. No longer allowed to e-mail her or text message her. If you do any of these things, I will seek a warrant for your arrest for telephonic harassment. You will be committing a crime of telephonic harassment. You are no longer welcome at her residence. You are not to be on her property or going through her garbage or any such activity. If you are found to be at her residence, you will be committing the crime of criminal trespass and I will seek a warrant for your arrest for that crime."

"I know you're just doing your job, Deputy Smith. Did Di tell you I went to her house and went through her garbage?"

"Yes, actually she did. You are simply not to contact her. If you want to challenge this then you can request a hearing. You need to contact the Multnomah County Courthouse for the filing instructions. Here's an official copy of the 'Restraining Order to Prevent Abuse.'"

"Thanks, and did you say your first name was Bob?"

"Yes."

"Bob Smith...I think that's the name of the Ashland Police sergeant who once was in charge of the D.A.R.E. Program at my kids' school."

"Yes, the Drug Abuse Resistance Program. In fact, I was once in charge of the program as well for the City of Tigard."

"No kidding?"

"Yeah, but the program in Tigard was determined to be ineffective, so after a few years the school district decided to stop funding it. However, while the program was in place, I got to drive a really cool, customized '69 Corvette."

"Really?"

"Yeah, it was a silver convertible we'd confiscated from a drug dealer."

"Wow! That sounds like that was a great gig for you. So are you related to the Ashland Bob Smith? I think he used to play that song called 'Total Eclipse of the Heart' for the climax of his presentation."

"Yeah, we used that same song but as far as I know, we're not related."

"Okay, well thanks for stopping by, officer. I'll make every effort to not contact Diane."

"Thank you for being cooperative and have a good day."

Right after Officer Smith left, I immediately called Tyler's store.

"It's a Great Day at CLEAR. This is Diane. How can I help you?"

"So this is the way you try to shut me up? Why did you call the cops on me? It's not good for my financial-advising business. Do you know how embarrassing it is to have a cop come to the office?"

"You *should* be embarrassed."

"Well, I'm going to challenge this and when the judge sees you don't have any grounds, this restraining order will get thrown out of court immediately."

"I wouldn't be so sure of that."

"Di, why do you keep playing these games? I don't want to play anymore."

"It's not a game to me and you deserved it."

"Di, why didn't you stay in Southern Oregon? You couldn't take the fact that Ty and I were resuming a normal relationship?"

"That's not it."

"Did you ever go see a counselor or a psychologist?"

"As a matter of fact I did, right after the second divorce."

"Are you still going?"

"I stopped. Dr. Hill was a little wacko. After she said I might have Borderline Personality Disorder, I ended the sessions."

"BPD? Isn't that what happens to women who were molested as kids, have drinking and drug problems, and cut themselves?"

"I don't know. I told you that the shrink was wacko."

"Yeah…but Diane…you've told me numerous times when we were married that you were molested as a kid, you've admitted to having drinking and drug problems, and didn't you tell me the reason you cut yourself below your neck when you were on that nature kick, was because you hated yourself for getting a boob job?"

"I'm calling the cops right now, since you've violated the restraining order."

"I'll see you in court, Diane."

She hung up.

A month later our court date was pretty uneventful. Di gave it a good effort, digging deep into the bowels of her high school drama classes with forced tears, choking, and a sporadically crackling voice. She tried to dig up things from fifteen years ago (or even more). She said in court she was scared because I "once threw her down the stairs" (she had slipped and fallen during one of her nightly drunken stupors). She also claimed I grasped her neck once (she had once connected fisticuffs with about three swings to my chops and my reflex was to naturally place my hands and arms out to create space. She was also drunk on that occasion). Multnomah County Judge Maureen McKnight was quick to point out to Di that her allegations needed to have "taken place in the previous 180 days," *not* in the last millennium.

Judge McKnight dismissed all charges.

CHAPTER 2:

Matthew Fox Stalking

Like father, like daughter. When it comes to writing, my daughter Faith is a chip off the old block and if it weren't for her recently revealing historical experiences regarding her mother, I probably wouldn't be caught up in *The Appeal of Stalking*. Therefore, the majority of this chapter is Faith's vantage point through her words of her own stalking experience...

Being the middle child has always been a challenge to me. My older sister, Libby, could never do anything wrong…at least in the eyes of our mother. It didn't help matters any that our mother would rather act like her sister, rather than our mother. Also, Mom spoiled my younger brother, Tyler, the baby. While growing up, anything my siblings wanted—designer clothes, video games, CD's, cars, etc.—all they had to do was ask, and our mother would always find a way to provide for them. Funny, but when I'd ask for things, which was a rarity, she'd always seem to be having financial problems, or she said I'd have to wait until pay day.

Dad, on the other hand, always tried to love the three kids in our family, equally. He didn't play favorites. For this reason, I have always tried to be pleasing to him. It was easy to give Dad attention and affection since I could never seem to get the same from my mother. So when I was asked for my stage name as a stripper, it was a no-brainer. Dad had written a novel called the *Goddess Seeker* about his affinity for the name "Jenny" and his admiration for Jens worldwide (and if I'm recalling correctly) Jenny McCarthy, Jennifer Connelly, and Jen Love. When I was asked my stage name by the club manager, naturally and effortlessly, "Jenny" rolled off my tongue.

It was an Indian summer night at Stars Cabaret in Bend, Oregon, the only exotic dancer gentlemen's club in town. There were three dancers on three stages, lap dances in a side area, and a designated V.I.P. area in the back of the club for gown dances and the shower stage. Clients bought me numerous drinks, and I remember thinking that Monde, tonight's deejay, was repeatedly playing some familiar music between sets...

> *Everybody wants to live (how they wanna live)*
> *And everybody wants to love (like they wanna love)*
> *And everybody wants to be...*
> *Closer to Free!*

The Bodeans' tune was the theme song from the nineties television show *Party of Five*.

> *Everybody wants respect (just a little bit)*
> *And everybody needs a chance (once in a while)*
> *Everybody wants to be...*
> *Closer to Free!*

Although the memory of the song's television show quickly disappeared, it returned eventually as I was preparing to go on stage. Damian the bouncer walked up next to me, pointed to the crowd, and said, "Jenny, who is that guy... at the back table?"

The club was dark and I was having trouble seeing anybody toward the back.

"I don't know. I can't tell. Why?"

"I think he's stalking you. He's been coming in here every night for a week and asking all sorts of questions about Jenny. He wants to know if Jenny has a townhouse behind Pilot Butte. He wants to know if Jenny has a young son, and if Jenny has a boyfriend?"

Yeah, yeah, yeah...
Everybody needs to touch (you know now and then)
And everybody wants a good good friend
Everybody wants to be...
Closer to Free...

As Monde transitioned the *Party of Five* music to Van Halen's "Spanked," one of Dad's favorites, instantly, as I started taking my place up on stage, a light flashed across to the back of the room and the same instant, a realization flashed in my mind.

It's Charlie!

The "Stalker" was the one-and-only Matthew Fox from *Party of Five* and Dr. Jack Shephard from *LOST*!

I looked over at him, winked, and flashed a flirtatious smile. By mid-song he had flung himself over my way, slamming a stack of hundreds onto the stage.

Tell me, who you going to call
When you need that affection?
Ya got to have it quick
Well, just a-hang your love line
In her direction, whoa
All you bad, bad boys
Call her up on the Spank Line...

I cranked up my efforts on the pole, spinning like there was no tomorrow. Holding myself upside down, touching the ceiling with my feet as my muscles in my ankles kept me alive as the blood rushed to my cheeks. My sequin-sparkling bra disappeared into the floor as all that remained was the matching G-string and six-inch acrylic pumps. Then, Van Halen turned into Eminem's "Same Song and Dance"...

> *Yeah baby do that dance*
> *It's the last dance you'll ever get the chance to do*
> *Girl shake that ass*
> *You ain't ever gonna break that glass, the windshield's*
> *too strong for you*
> *I said, Yeah baby sing that song*
> *It's the last song you'll ever get the chance to sing*
> *You sexy little thing...*

I floated off the pole and into Matthew's presence. Everything was surreal. "Charlie" was not only my favorite, he was MOM's favorite. Every Wednesday night in the mid-nineties the family would gather together for one hour of television: Mom, Dad, Libby, Tyler and me. It was our one hour of weekly peace, since Mom spent nearly all of the other 167 hours nagging Dad. I guess she took that hour to lust after Matthew. And now, here I was, getting naked, slamming my boobs and shaking my ass in the face of Mom's Fantasy Man, while I swept close to a couple thousand dollars from him and onto the stage for ten minutes of dancing. This entire experience was in SLOW MOTION...

Matthew was dressed casually, with designer jeans and a long-sleeved, un-tucked collared shirt and T-shirt underneath. I also noticed he was wearing Nike AIR 360 running shoes.

The funny thing is, I don't know if Dad ever knew Matthew was Mom's Dream Man.

Now, Matthew was about to complete filming on the final season of *LOST*, the biggest television show ever, and Dad was a HUGE Jack Shepherd fan and *LOST* expert. In fact, Dad even went to Australia in March 2008 because he was searching for his long-lost Aussie pen pal, and he said this wasn't unlike the scene from the *LOST* episode, "The Constant"... Dad and I watched the scene together online in which Desmond and Penny reconnected after eight years and it honestly brought tears to our eyes and it's one of the few times Dad and I have cried together. Dad told me the story about how he wanted to go in 2001 to see his Aussie angel; he'd even bought the plane ticket. Mom cried to the D.A. that Dad shouldn't be allowed to go. She claimed he was trying to skip the country and not pay child and spousal support, so the D.A. swallowed her crap and didn't allow Dad to renew his passport. That was so wrong. Mom was the one who wanted the divorce, yet she didn't want anyone else to have Dad. She never wanted Dad to be free when all he's ever wanted was to escape. It's always been creepy. Like Mom was stalking Dad when they were kids, while they were married, and she's still been stalking him since they divorced.

After Eminem's song ended, and after I had picked up my lingerie, the cash, and placed it in my purse, I looked up and noticed Matthew motioning for me to come over to his table in the back of the room. I got dressed and then approached him. He pulled out a chair for me and reached his hand toward me. As our hands touched, electricity shot through my soul.

"I'm Matthew."

"Matthew Fox. I know. I'm Jenny...or actually, I'm Faith."

"It's a pleasure to meet you, Faith."

"It's a pleasure to meet you, Charlie...uhhh Jack, or, I mean Matthew."

We both laughed.

"We know what you mean...may I order you a drink?" he asked as Brittney the waitress approached to take our order.

"What can I get you two?"

"I'd like a vodka/cran," I said.

"I'll have another Tanqueray and tonic," said Matthew.

"Will do," said Brittney.

"You are quite the performer," said Matthew. "Why are you dancing in Central Oregon?"

"I've only been doing this for a few weeks. Bend just seemed like a good place to try it."

"Do you know if you were dancing in Vegas or Dallas, you would make a killing? Your personality, athleticism, and beauty are rare combinations. If this is something you want to make a career out of, you should really think about going where the money is."

"Thanks, and I'll keep that in mind. Actually, I'm just getting some space from my mom. We had a falling out."

"So sorry. What happened? Oh, you don't really have to tell me if you don't want to."

"No, Matthew. It's all right. A couple things happened. I was living down in Ashland at the time. She brought a teenager to my home on the Fourth of July against my wishes, and then she slept with him on my five-year-old son's new bed."

"Damn…so your mom's a cougar?"

"Yeah. My mom's almost fifty, going on fourteen. Her best friend Hanna is forty-something and she's been chasing the young boys for years. They're both on the prowl with their friend, Angie. Most people call her Angina. Angina likes to make and consume decorated cakes, so she's packed on quite a few pounds lately. She's backed off chasing the young guys, since they don't want to touch her anymore, so now it's just mostly Mom and Hanna who are pouncing on the innocent young men. Sorry for rambling."

"That's okay. I just hope your mom's teenager wasn't under eighteen?"

"I don't think he was but it wouldn't be the first time she's committed statutory rape."

"I think it's okay for there to be an age difference, as long as you aren't breaking the law."

"I agree. But she's always been good at getting away with things like that."

"Wow."

"And if she doesn't get what she wants, she's a pro at pouring on the Christian guilt."

"How so?"

"She'd have a field day if she knew I was stripping. She'd be dumping on me how terrible of a person, a daughter, a mother, and a bad Christian I am for dancing."

"Exotic dancing is an art form. Stripping is not against the law. It's not drug dealing, it's not prostitution, it's not statutory rape, it's not child molestation, it's not harassment or stalking…it's LEGAL! And besides, Christ opened his arms to everyone, especially beautiful women!"

"The funny thing is, dancing at one time in her life would have been Mom's dream job. All she's ever seemed to care about are her looks and her weight. It's always been a sad situation."

"It sounds like it."

"Enough of that. I just want to tell you that *Party of Five* had a huge impact on me while I was growing up, particularly in my adolescence."

"Thank you. On a certain level everybody can relate to a show about a family trying to stay together."

"Isn't that the truth? Matthew, you seem very sweet and if I might say…your personality reminds me a lot like Charlie's from the show."

"I've heard that before so I guess I'll take that as a compliment."

"Indeed it is."

As Brittney brought us our drinks, I began pondering how Matthew was amazingly shy, cute and polite. I had to remind myself that even though this moment was starting to seem like a fairy tale, I was still at work…

"Would you like a private dance?"

He looked away and then back at me with the smirk that's melted millions of American women during much of the previous two decades.

"I suppose you could twist my arm."

I returned his smile, then took Matthew's hand and led him to the private dance area. This moment seemed crazy and I thought about what Mom would think if she saw me now, dancing for Charlie…

I had barely begun dancing when Matthew grabbed my arm and said, "Look, I get private dances all the time when I come to strip clubs, but there is something about you. I don't want to make you do it. You seem like a REAL person…not a stripper. Here, sit down beside me and let's just talk."

"Whatever you want, Matthew. Ian, the club manager, says I have to charge you twenty dollars per song."

"I don't care about the money. I'll pay you a hundred bucks a song. What are you really doing here?"

"A couple weeks ago, I was in a jam to make rent. My son and I were going to get evicted, so I did it one time and the money was so good that I decided to keep doing it."

"What about the kid's father? Doesn't he help you out?"

"That's the thing. Erasmo is an illegal alien, he's been deported once already, and he has paid very little. The state says he owes me twenty thousand by now."

"Does he have a job?"

"He works under the table pouring concrete and he sells pot and God knows what other drugs. I really don't want to have anything to do with drugs or someone who sells them. It's so disgraceful that my son's father is a dealer."

"I told you that you're a real person. You're not really a stripper."

"The reason I seem like a real person is because my Dad and his parents raised me better. I know I might never get to see you again so I want to tell you what you and your show *Party of Five* had on me as a kid, so hear me out."

"Okay."

"My family never did anything together without my parents fighting. We rarely ever even ate dinner together as a family, but for one hour a week we would all watch *Party of Five* together. From the time I was nine years old until just before I turned Sweet Sixteen, Wednesday night at nine p.m. was the time I looked forward to every week."

"You really did grow up with the show, didn't you?"

"You were a great role model, Charlie. What your broken family had in that show was something that all children deserve to have from their parents. In the show, the Salinger family lost their parents to a drunk driver, but you rallied. You had your disagreements but you were all team players and you came to the table and talked through and worked through your problems. I'm sorry for my tears."

"Faith, it means a lot that you are expressing your feelings about the show. Did you know that the show was scheduled to be cancelled after the first season?"

"No way, Matthew."

"Yes, but somehow the show won the Golden Globe for Best Drama, the network reconsidered, and the rest is history."

At that point I was embarrassed for getting so emotional so I tried to shift gears into humor.

"Did you ever hook up with Jennifer Love Hewitt?"

"No," he laughed.

"Did you come here with some of your buddies?"

"Yeah," he said. "My manager, Ronnie, and a couple of new friends we made downtown at the Deschutes Brewery."

"Do you want to go rejoin them?"

"Sure, but why don't you come along and I'll introduce you to them."

Matthew took my hand and led me back to the main area of the club. He genuinely seemed to be enjoying my company.

When we returned to the table, two of the guys hanging out with Matthew had moved to the stage. One remained as we approached.

"Faith, this is Ronnie, my manager," said Matthew.

Ronnie reached out his hand. "Pleased to meet you, Faith. It's about time Matt got to meet you. Did you know he's been stalking you for at least a week?"

"Huh?" I laughed. "That's what Damian, the bouncer said!"

"Don't believe everything Ronnie tells you, Faith," said Matthew.

"How long have you been Matthew's manager, Ronnie?"

"We've been best friends since Wyoming, where we grew up together. It's my job to keep him out of trouble."

"With the ladies?"

"Exactly, Faith!"

Monde switched the music to another Emimen song. This time he chose "Mom"…

> *My mom loved Valium and lots of drugs*
> *That's why I am like I am 'cause I'm like her*
> *Because my mom loved Valium and lots of drugs*
> *That's why I'm on what I'm on 'cause I'm my mom*

"Faith, I'm a big Eminem fan," said Matthew. "I love *RELAPSE*, the new album."

"I love it too!" I said. Then I joined into singing the song…

> *Valium was in everything, food that I ate*
> *The water that I drank, fuckin' peas in my plate*
> *She sprinkled just enough of it to season my steak*
> *So every day I have at least three stomach aches*

"Ronnie! Isn't she awesome? This girl can sing Eminem, line for line."

Then Matthew chimed in and sang some of the lines, himself…

> *Now tell me what kind of mother would want to see her*
> *son grow up to be an under-a-fuckin'-chiever?*
> *My teacher didn't think I was gonna be nothin' either*
> *"What the fuck you stickin' gum up under the fuckin' seat*
> *for?"*
> *"Mrs. Mathers, your son has been huffin' ether*
> *Either that or the motherfucker's been puffin' reefer"*

The drinks and the laughter continued to flow. Matthew then leaned over and whispered into my ear. "Do you want to come over to my place when your shift ends?"

"Sure," I replied. "I'd like that, but I need to check in with my sitter and make sure my son is okay and sleeping."

After texting and receiving a reply from my friend, Courtney, who was watching my son, I had the green light for a rendezvous with Matthew Fox.

"Matthew, I will meet you but my boss has made it clear that I can't break the rules of hanging out with customers."

"I understand," he said. "But doesn't tonight seem like destiny? I've been looking for someone like you for a long time. I think we're supposed to continue."

"I have about two more hours. Then I can meet you."

Matthew took a pen from his pocket, grabbed a napkin from the table and wrote something on it before handing it to me.

"Here, call me when you want me."

"Thank you, talk to you soon."

I walked to the break room in the back and immediately put Matthew's number and address into my phone.

"Jenny!" said the bouncer.

"Damian, what are you doing following me?"

"I need to take that napkin from you. We have rules, you know."

"Yeah. Okay, here it is, I don't want it. I know I shouldn't be hanging out with customers, especially the ones who are here stalking the girls."

Two hours later, I had finished my shift and used the mapping app in my iPhone to guide me to Matthew's home. It was on the west side of Bend, not far from Summit High School. For being a big star, I thought it was a bit odd that his home appeared to be a modest house in a modest neighborhood.

There were three other guys inside the front door when I entered.

"Hi Jenny…errr, Faith," yelled Ronnie. "Matt's getting some drinks. Come on in. Do you know Corey Moore and Mark Happe?"

"I think I've seen you guys in the club."

Corey and Mark had crazed looks on their faces with some white powder on their faces.

They each had razor blades and they started snorting lines from mirrors off the dining room table.

"Do you want some blow, Faith?" asked Ronnie.

"Where did you get it?" I asked.

"From Corey, of course," said Matthew. "He has the best coke in Bend. Here's a vodka/cran for you, Faith, and Hennessey on the rocks for the rest of us. We're out of gin."

Damn, this was a dilemma. I don't want to look like a prude, I thought. I've only seen cocaine one other time in my life, in Ashland when I was in high school at a party with my softball teammates. Many of my friends took it and most of the time they didn't seem to have a problem.

"Happe, give Faith your straw," said Ronnie. "Are you ready for some nose candy?"

Mark started to hand it to me. I took the straw from him and then Corey handed me the razor blade as he poured some of the coke from a vial and onto the mirror in front of me.

"I've never done this before," I said. I was starting to feel incredibly nervous and pressured.

"It's a trip," said Matthew. "The journey is the destination."

"Matthew, I hate that saying. My mom always says that."

"Oh…Sorry."

I pulled myself together and even though it was against my better judgment, as I was about to place the straw next to the line, I waved my hair back over one of my shoulders. As I looked up at the ceiling, I actually saw my grandma's face…I immediately sat up and dropped the straw.

"I can't do this."

"Are you sure?" asked Ronnie.

"I just don't want to."

"It's okay, Faith," said Matthew as he moved in next to me. "Here, I'll do a line for you and for me."

After Matthew finished inhaling two lines he looked up with some wildness in his eyes and said, "Here, let's go into the living room."

I still couldn't believe I had just watched Charlie, a.k.a. Dr. Jack Shephard, a.k.a. Matthew Fox, doing drugs. This really was a trip! He gently took my hand again into his as he had in the club. We left the other three behind, walked out of the dining room and then to the couch. He sat down next to me and picked up an acoustic guitar.

He started to play the guitar and I was impressed with his talents. Instantly, even though Matthew sang some variations on the words, it sounded like he was attempting to play a popular classic song by the Black Crowes...

"She never mentions the word addiction...
in certain company...
Yes, she'll tell you she saves African orphans
after she fucks up her family"...

I instantly became mesmerized by Matthew's musical talent. The next thing I knew, I was standing up, eyes closed, now dancing and swaying to his sweet singing... and the next song was a classic Hootie song with the same theme as the Crowes' one...

"She never lets me in
only tells me where she's been
when she's had too much to drink
I say that I don't care, I just run my hands
through her dark hair then I pray to God
you gotta help me fly away
And just...
Let her cry... if the tears fall down like rain
Let her sing... if it eases all her pain

Let her go... let her walk right out on me
And if the sun comes up tomorrow
Let her be... let her be"...

The song was so freely flowing that I didn't even notice Matthew pitching his guitar to Ronnie in the middle and Ronnie didn't even miss a beat on the guitar, or in the words.

Matthew moved into me and we started dancing closely. It was beautiful. We were free and I felt like tonight was a dream...

The moment was so magical. Matthew led me into his bedroom and whispered into my ear, "May I take your nipple rings out?"

"Huh?" I replied.

"You don't really need them. When I saw them at the club, that's the first thing I told myself I was going to help you with."

"Really, Matthew, you'd do that for me?"

"Sure."

"It's not necessary but if you want to..."

Almost effortlessly as the music continued, Matthew pulled a pair of needle-nose pliers off the top of his dresser and within a few seconds, he had not only removed my top, but the rings were also magically gone immediately and I didn't feel a thing.

The rest of the night was completely natural. Being with Charlie-Jack-Matthew Fox was like a dream come true. He was incredibly gentle and kind. His wonderful smile was hypnotic, just like millions of people see on television every week.

The lovemaking was incredible. We started out with passionate kissing. Matthew slid his hand behind my neck, pulled me close and kissed me like I knew at that very moment, that I was the only woman on the planet for him. The experience with him was something I will remember forever and if any other woman had the chance to be in my shoes, she would be lying if she said she wouldn't give her all for America's Sexiest Man Alive.

By the time we were finished releasing our hearts and souls to one another, my face and hair were drenched with sweat, like a good varsity volleyball conditioning workout when I played for Ashland High!

As we rested, Matthew put his hand on the side of my face and stared deeply into my eyes. I might be somewhat naïve, but not naïve enough to know that he was not in love with me. However, the way he touched me so gently and displayed such compassion I'd compare to a familiar performance of Charlie on *Party of Five*. I admit it was difficult to decide whether or not I was making love with a television character, or a man who discovered that he was living in the same town as me.

In the closing moments, I wondered why he was being so respectful when in his eyes I felt that he could view me the same way I was viewed by most of the customers at Stars. I'm just another stupid, ditzy stripper who has no respect for herself, and has nothing to offer a man like him.

He wrapped his arms around me and then we spooned and then I turned over facing him as we cuddled. Matthew looked into my eyes again and said, "That was incredible. I've never been with a woman like you before, Faith."

"Don't give me that, Dr. Jack Shephard. I'm sure you say that to all your Hollywood girls."

"I'm serious," he said. "I could barely keep up with you. Where do you get all of your stamina, endurance and energy?"

"Probably from my dad. He runs marathons and does triathlons."

"No wonder."

We fell asleep in each other's arms for a few hours. As the sun was starting to come up, I woke up and knew I needed to go. I tried not to wake Matthew up as I got out of bed, and got dressed but to no avail.

"Faith, can you stay?" he asked.

"I'm afraid I need to go."

"What would it take to get you to stay?"

I started howling with laughter. "Well, you can start by telling me how *LOST* ends?"

"Actually, I possibly could. Right now the producers have three endings they're trying to choose from. I have my favorite but the jury is still out. We can talk about that later. You would just have to promise not to tell a soul, or I'd have to kill you. In the meantime, how about one of my killer Greek omelets?"

"I'd love to stay, but I need to get to my son before he wakes up. Maybe I can have a rain check?"

"Of course. I'll call you."

Since Matthew was still in bed, I bent over to him and we exchanged a nice, parting kiss.

He got up, tied a towel around himself and walked me to the door.

"Faith. Thanks for last night. I'll talk to you soon."

"Thank you, Matthew. I had a great time."

After one final hug and kiss, I got in my car and drove home.

Matthew called later that day to ask me how I was feeling and say that he would be leaving tomorrow for Hawaii to begin shooting the final season of *LOST*. He said he'd be back in "a few months" and we could get together again; do a real date, with "dinner and a movie." I wished him good luck with his work and thanked him for a memorable night.

I kept really busy after that night, with permanently moving to Central Oregon, work and raising my son. I also detached myself from my mother since she had tried to take my son again to try to raise him on her own. As a result the weeks flew by and before I knew it, the holiday season had already come and gone. I admit, I spent some of my time researching Mr. Fox during the fall, and I discovered that he was actually married and planned to move his wife and two boys to Bend since *LOST* was going to be his final work in television. His family would be bidding farewell to their Hawaiian home of the previous six television years.

From the interviews I'd read, it sounded like Matthew was focusing on being the All-American family man. I thus resolved that our earlier rendezvous was going to become a pleasant dream, a great story. Almost a fiction that one would find in one of thousands of romance novels my lonely mother loves to read on her back porch, amidst the cigarette smoke of many frigid nights.

I was wrong. Déjà vu came at the end of December. Monde once again played *Closer to Free* as I walked out of the changing room, and as I shook my head and smiled. Sure enough, there was Matthew in his familiar seat at the back of the club. We instantly made eye contact and he waved me over.

Here we go again, I thought.

"Hey stranger," I said.

"Jenny…errr…Faith, I was hoping you'd still be here."

"When did you get back?"

"Just yesterday. I spent Christmas with at my parents in Wyoming."

"What about your family…particularly your wife?"

"O, Margherita was there."

"Where's she at tonight?"

"Home with the kids."

"And Matthew, what about the tabloids and the Internet?"

"Listen, Faith, I make it a strict policy never to look at anything on the Internet that pertains to me personally or to anything I'm working on."

"There've been rumors that the cab drivers might call the tabloids."

"Baby, no need to be alarmed. If any journalists ask me if I've had an affair with a stripper, I'll simply say that the story is not true and I'm not going to comment on it."

"Okay, Matthew, does Mrs. Fox know where her husband is right now?"

"Yeah, we've been married a long time. She knows I am a man, and I am an appreciator of women who needs to be free sometimes and unwind. With the pressure I'm under as a performer, she lets me do what I want in order to relax."

"So you're in an *Open Relationship?*"

"That's what we call it."

"I just want to be clear what's going on."

"Sure. Do you have plans tonight?"

"I'm not sure."

"Faith, I've missed you. I was hoping we could go somewhere to be alone."

"Okay, I need to work at least a couple hours. My friend, Andi, with Checker Cab can take you to my place at midnight."

"That sounds perfect to me."

"She'll be out front waiting for you. I'm going to leave at 11:30. Matthew, we can't leave together, or this time I really will get fired!"

"Whatever you say."

So at 11:30 Andi picked me up in her cab with another stripper, my friend Cherry.

I had texted Andi earlier to take Cherry home first, and then drop me off before she headed back to pick up Matthew. I also texted Andi not to say anything to Cherry about Matthew, since she'd probably be jealous and tell the manager and I'd be done.

After Andi picked us up, as a safety precaution to be sure none of the clients were followed, she took numerous turns through downtown Bend prior to heading to Cherry's home.

We were about to discover that on this night, Andi wasn't quick enough.

"Girls," Andi said. "I hate to tell you this, but there's a car that's been following us since the club."

"What the hell?" I said.

"Fucking stalker!" said Cherry. "I need to get home, Andi. I'll kick his ass if he tries to pull anything."

Andi pulled onto Colt Lane and arrived in the general vicinity of Cherry's house.

"He's still with us, Cherry," said Andi. "Maybe I should just drive around the area until he leaves."

"Just stop, Andi," said Cherry. "He can't be that stupid not to know that the cab driver wouldn't call the cops."

Cherry got out of the cab. Even though it was dark, it looked like the stalker was driving a silver BMW.

Just then a man flew out of the car and stumbled towards the cab.

Cherry must have realized who it was because she dashed back and opened my door, while laughing.

"FAITH, Don't LOOK NOW…But it's…MATTHEW FOX STALKING!"

"Oh shit," I said.

Matthew got in the back of the cab and immediately started groping me.

"You two know each other?" asked Cherry.

"I guess it looks like we do." I said. "Actually, my family knows him, but please don't say anything, okay, Cherry?"

"Of course not," she laughed.

Cherry paid Andi her portion of the cab fare, and we pulled away.

"Matthew, that was creepy," I said. "You looked like a stalker."

"Faith, I was afraid you were just going to blow me off," said Matthew.

"Why would I do that, Matthew?"

"Faith, I didn't want to take any chances of losing you. I've missed you while I've been gone."

"But what were you doing? I told you Andi would pick you up at midnight."

"I don't know. I must have just lost my head."

"Matthew, if I get fired for this, it's not going to be good."

"Listen Faith, you don't need to be dancing. I've been doing a lot of thinking and I want to get you out of there. I'm setting up a bank account for you and your boy. I want you to quit dancing. I'll take care of everything."

After I spent another night with Matthew, his idea of "taking care of everything" meant that he'd disappear. I've yet to hear from him since.

I thus decided to get proactive and call my dad and tell him what happened.

As a result of our conversations, the following is *The National Enquirer* story Dad wrote under the ghostwriter's name of "Joe North." I hit the jackpot, earning $300,000 for the interview, and Dad cashed in with $100,000 for writing it. Dad earned a degree from journalism school at the University of Oregon for a reason, and does anybody out there know what sports writers or high school journalism teachers make these days? The good ones do not get paid what they are worth! If making hundreds of thousands of dollars for this kind of story makes my dad my "pimp," then so be it. If the fact my dad hired high-profile attorney Gloria Allred who then negotiated a separate payment for a story with *InTouch Magazine* and this means that Dad "pimped me out," then so be it. We live in America for chrissakes. Dad and I are a team. We capitalized on the opportunity. That's why they call it Capitalism. If some of my family and friends still don't get this, they need to go back to school and take a business class and maybe even a history class. It's the beauty of living in the Land of the Free and the Home of the Brave. And remember, the published version of the following story was edited so even though it's close, it's not word for word to this one. I believe everyone deserves to see the original story. Readers should also remember not to always believe everything they see in the tabloids...

Matthew Fox Sex Scandal

Matthew Fox's squeaky-clean image as a family man could soon be *"LOST"* for good after he was caught up in a cheating scandal involving a tattooed stripper.

The stripper, young enough to be his daughter, claims she began an affair with the 43-year-old star – who plays Dr. Jack Shephard – after meeting him at a strip club in Bend, Ore.

Faith Freeman, 25, who danced at the Stars Cabaret club in Bend, confessed to the ENQUIRER: "Yes, I've been having an affair with Matthew Fox. We've been intimate together.

"I've got to be careful what I say. Even though at first, I didn't know he was married, he is, and he has kids. I've kept voice mails, text messages and the photos he has sent me."

Faith has told others of her incredible boast about her alleged sexual exploits with the actor.

What's more, an eyewitness claims to have seen Fox making out with Faith in the back of a cab. "I've driven Matthew Fox to Stars numerous times," claims Checker Cab driver Andi Watson. "Although he's nice like on television, I got this creepy feeling about him, almost like he was a stalker.

"After he had gotten together with Faith, my mind became at ease on the drives to his place."

The actor vehemently denies that he has had a relationship with Faith. But on recent trips to Bend, Fox has reportedly behaved like a fox in the henhouse – flirting with women at the Stars strip club, according to locals.

"Matthew's partying is out of control. He's boozing and carrying on with women but the only one I've seen him leave with is Faith," revealed a source.

"His carousing is at an all-time high since he bought a house in Bend," said Karla Mackey, another driver for Checker Cab. "I don't know how long his marriage can last."

"I heard that the bouncers in the strip clubs have strict orders to watch carefully and make sure no girls leave with him," said another source. "Apparently, Faith has been the exception."

A friend of Faith's claimed that they have dated on a number of occasions. "The first time was in September and he's been back monthly with the last time being on December 29."

"I did not know Matthew was married until the last time we dated," Faith explained. "At first, I admit I was a little star-struck when we met. Besides, Matthew Fox will forever be my mom's fantasy dream guy, ever since the show *Party of Five*.

"Mom and I have been at odds since she's tried to take custody of my son numerous times over the years, her latest vain attempt being in August. In addition, my son's dad is a deadbeat illegal alien, so I had to take matters into my own hands by moving to Bend and finding a job in which I could earn enough to pay the bills and support my boy.

"Anyway, if Mom hadn't been acting so unsupportive and bitchy lately, I probably would have fixed her up with Matthew since she's on the prowl for husband #3 right now.

"But instead, I decided to keep Matthew for myself. Next time, Mom might want to treat me nicer."

The Stars club management found out about Faith's dates with Matthew. She was suspended and then fired.

"The last time Matthew came into the club, he was with his friends and they all talked with Faith, who dances under the name 'Jenny'," said a source.

"Matthew paid $100 to see Faith and another girl perform a shower set for him. Two naked girls go into a shower and sponge each other down while the customer watches."

"Then he took a $20 lap dance in the back of the club and he slipped a note to Faith to meet him in the cab when the bouncer wasn't watching."

She left the club in a taxi with another girl but then the other girl got out and Fox jumped in next to Faith, claimed Faith's friend.

Checker Cab's Andi Watson confirmed she drove the couple on Dec. 29.

"Faith is gorgeous, but she's a mess. She's tall with blonde hair and tattoos on her shoulder and ankles," said Andi, who knows Faith and has frequently driven the exotic dancer around Bend.

"The first time I drove her home after she had been out with him, Faith just kept telling me, 'It's Matthew Fox, it's Matthew Fox. I grew up with him.'

"After getting in the cab, Fox was kind of quiet, just sitting there, sometimes laughing at the things Faith was saying," said Andi.

"He was wearing casual, all-designer clothes, a blue jacket and a nice white shirt and jeans. He had his usual short haircut, but a couple of days' growth of beard.

"They kissed and touched each other in the cab. I took them to Faith's townhouse, and they told me to pick them up in an hour and a half.

"When I got back they both came out and got back into the cab. Surprisingly, they were more romantic than before – kissing a lot more and hugging each other.

"I drove him home and he jumped out, kissing Faith good night and telling her, 'That was fun. I'll see you soon.'

"He had me drop him off two blocks from his home. He said, 'I told my wife I was going out with the guys. I can't afford to let her see a girl in the cab.'

"Then Faith had me drive her to her babysitter's house to pick up her five-year-old son.

Although it was the middle of the night, she told me she had to make a call on her cell phone.

"Then to my amazement, she began bragging to a pal, 'I just hooked up with Matthew Fox. We did it five times in my bed.'"

After five years on *LOST*, Fox has pledged in interviews to move to Oregon to spend quality time with his wife of 18 years, Margherita, 42, and their two children, ages 11 and 8.

Sounding like a true romantic, the star confided to one magazine that he often tells his wife in Italian: "I love you more than anything in the world."

Ironically, his wild side allegedly exploded to the surface in Bend – the very town where he plans to move his family.

When confronted by *The ENQUIRER*, Faith initially admitted she had been having a sexual affair with Matthew Fox. But soon after, the stripper hired celebrity lawyer Gloria Allred to attempt to sell her story and refused to cooperate further apart from saying, "Matthew said he'd take care of everything after I was fired at the end of December," said Faith. "I'm still waiting to hear from him."

How *LOST* ends (conclusion 1 of 3)...

This is what Matthew Fox told me in late December 2009, would be his choice of endings for America's Greatest Television Drama, EVER. This ending is his "personal favorite" even though some critics might find a comparison to the ending of "The Sopranos"...

There are six cast members who step away from the crowd on the beach. Jack, Hurley, Kate, Claire, Sawyer, and (possibly) Locke (but the final one is still up in the air)...

The scene cuts away to someone pulling a record album from a shelf (I think it might be Desmond) and putting it on a turntable and starting the record by turning on the player and putting the needle onto it.

Each of the characters then take turns starting to draw, then finishing, one of the following LARGE letters or numbers in the sand on the beach. The music continues to play as this is done...

E-5-C-4-P-3

It's the song from the record album called *Escape* by Journey.

The camera pans above to show the word "E5C4P3" in LARGE LETTERS in the sand.

The sky starts to glow as in earlier episodes when the time would change...but this time the glow is from a spaceship...

It's the Scarab Beatle Spaceship from the album...it hovers and then lands on the beach...next to where the people have spelled E5C4P3 in the sand... It's unclear but the smoke monster might have transformed somehow into the scarab beetle. A ramp descends from underneath the spaceship. The cast loads onto the ship, the ramp rises, and the spaceship flies into the stars...

Snippets of the song that are heard in the background as these events unfold are...

Now he's leavin', getting out from this masquerade
Oh gotta go
I'm finally out in the clear and I'm free
I've got dreams I'm livin' for
I'm movin' on where they'll never find me
Rollin' on to anywhere

I'll break away, yes I'm on my way
Leavin' today, yes I'm on my way
Runnin' scared can change your mind
I never knew I had so much to give
How hard times can fool ya
I'm leaving, leavin' today
Yes, I'm on my way
This is my Escape
Yes, I'm on my way, I'll break away...

Saying my daughter, Faith, has been "unlucky in love" would be an understatement. I know dads usually don't approve of the men whom their daughters take an interest in, and she's gone from both ends of the spectrum...deadbeat illegal alien to America's Top Television Superstar...Next time, I hope she'll shoot for somewhere in the middle and strive for someone more peaceful—an American citizen, Oregon Ducks' fan, who hasn't spent any time in prison and doesn't have this experience on his Bucket List.

I don't think this is too much for a dad to ask.

CHAPTER 3:

Stalking the Grandmother

After the Matthew Fox story was released worldwide, things apparently became a little rough for the ex-wife. She had moved back to Ashland, and as expected, immediately became reclusive after the *National Enquirer* coverage. If she did venture out to get her smokes, she had to explain herself to her friends. That must have been rough since she had no idea any of this was coming. Diane desperately attempted to patch things up with Faith as a means to simply being "in the know." Faith wouldn't have any of this since her mom didn't give a rat's ass about her, having not made contact with her for more than seven months, including in November for Faith's birthday or Christmas.

As a result, Diane and the other two kids posted a biting statement on their Facebook pages:

Re: Our sister…
We'd like to ask that all of you show respect for our family as we deal with this situation. The decisions that were made to create drama and sensationalism do not represent us, or who we are today. What we have here is simply a case of a father taking advantage of an alcoholic, drug-addicted daughter for the financial benefits which are a result of unnecessary hype and the resulting fiction which has followed.

People, Faith is sick. She's not the Faith we all once loved. However, before you speak negatively of her, or the situation, we'd challenge everyone to remember that there is a five-year-old boy sitting in her presence and he is suffering.

This is all we wish to say on the topic. We appreciate all of your support through texts and calls but please respect our privacy as we are burnt out on this topic.

Tyler, Libby, Diane

Of all of my kids, Faith has always been the most sensitive. After the Matthew Fox story was released, she knew there would be backlash through online comments. They were brutal. Later in July, while she was running in Medford, ironically she passed out on the lawn of the Department of Human Services. I discovered that she'd followed into her mother's alcoholic footsteps as she tipped the breathalyzer at 0.22.

"Dad, I'm in the hospital," Faith said, via telephone.

"What happened?" I replied.

"I got heatstroke and was dehydrated while running."

"Haven't I warned you not to be running in the heat of the day in Medford? It almost hit 110 down there today."

"I know. You were right. I blew it."

"Did you call your mom?"

"I did."

"Oh shit, is she coming to see you?"

"I don't know. Sounds like she's busy watching her boyfriend's toddlers. Dad, I have to tell you something. I was drunk and someone from the Department of Human Services called the ambulance."

"Oh shit. You were drinking again, and then you went running?"

"Yeah. I've just been so stressed out. You know, Dad, ever since the Fox story was published I can't go anywhere without people harassing me, stalking me, and practically mauling me wanting to talk about it."

"Faith, you know what this means, now?"

"I think so."

"Your mom's going to try to take your kid away from you again."

"I know. She's probably already in the DHS office at this moment."

Six weeks later, the grandmother had successfully kidnapped the grandson. She worked the system. She worked things so that personnel from the local Department of Human Services (DHS) had opened an investigation. As a result, Faith would not be allowed to take her son out of Southern Oregon until the investigation was complete. Grandma Diane teamed up with Erasmo and immediately registered Trystan for the first grade. The problem I had with this was that the kid had been in preschool the previous year.

Skipping kindergarten is like skipping Christmas…

It should never happen.

One of my favorite books is by Robert Fulghum, *All I Really Need to Know I Learned in Kindergarten.* Although I could forgive Erasmo for not having read this book, not only had Diane not read it, she must have also skipped kindergarten because that's exactly what she had the grandson, Trystan, do.

Maybe that's why she doesn't play by the rules. Maybe that's why she doesn't *"share everything, play fair(ly), clean up her own mess, or say she's sorry when she hurts somebody."* Maybe that's why she "hits people, takes things that aren't hers," and doesn't deal with her father and stepbrother molesting her during her childhood?

I called Tyler to see if he would talk some sense into his mom and immediately request that they return the kid to the appropriate placement, in school… kindergarten!

"Why are you calling me?"

"Son, we need to talk about your mom having Trystan skip kindergarten. The poor kid is going to be lost in first grade."

"You are a horrible father."

"Ty, have you taken the rude and mean-spirited attempt at an essay toward Faith off your Facebook page?"

"Not yet, and I don't plan on it."

"Son, you can think what you want of me, which hurts. But until you know what's been going on and the history of all of these years, you should never rush to judgment."

"You are a horrible father."

"Son, I think I'm going to end this phone conversation before it gets started."

"Dad, I'm not surprised."

"On second thought, Son, I think we'd have a better chance getting somewhere if we do this face to face."

"Why should I want to meet with you?"

"Son, are you afraid of your Dad?"

"Hell no, Dad. I'll meet you but I want to pick the spot."

"Doesn't matter to me where we talk, Son, only that we do it. Where and when would you like to meet?"

"George's."

"George's?"

"Dancin' Bear. Six tonight."

"All right. See you there."

After a Google search I discovered that *George's Dancin' Bear* was actually *George's Dancin' B-A-R-E,* a strip club in North Portland just off Interstate Avenue and Columbia Boulevard. When your son tends to have a hard enough time communicating, a beggar can't be a chooser for a meeting location. I've never been to a strip bar with my son before, but I guess there is always a first time for everything.

When I entered the *Dancin' Bare* at 6:05 p.m., I could see Tyler sitting at the bar with a large draft pitcher and two glasses. He waved me over. I noticed three girls performing on stages with blasting hip hop music in the background.

"Can you ever make it on time, Dad?" he said as he filled the two glasses.

"I'm sorry, Son, for being five minutes late. Traffic from Beaverton is a little crazy this time of the day."

"Hell, I run all over this city and I make my appointments on time."

"I'm proud of you, Son. Now, can you drink and talk at the same time?"

"Sure."

I lifted my glass. "Here's to you, Sonshine."

"Cheers," he said as he lifted his glass to mine.

"Does Holly approve of you meeting with your dad in strip bars?"

"She lets me be free to be me."

"I like that, Son, but your mother would have a shit-fit if she knew we were here."

"That's nothing we have to worry about, Dad."

"She threw me out of the house for three months when I went to Robb Romeo's bachelor party in '95."

"You deserved that, Dad."

"But it's okay for us to be here, today?"

"Sure. Times have changed. Women have figured things out. I'm going to marry Holly someday, and maybe then I'll decide not to come to places like this."

"Son, you know I think the world of Holly. She's so talented, kind, and intelligent."

"Sometimes, Dad, I wonder what she sees in me."

"Why do you say that?"

"Well, I didn't end up getting a college education, like she did. I know that was a big deal to you as well, Dad."

"Nahhh, Holly loves you for you, and sees into your core and your passion and drive. You are defying the odds, Son, by kicking ass in business with the two or three college terms you did finish. There are a lot of college grads out here in this economy who either can't find a job or have to start at minimum wage. You're a living example of where dedication, determination, and desire can take you."

"Thanks, Dad. That means a lot and I owe you a lot of the credit for showing me how to endure and keep my eyes on goals."

"No. Thank you, Son. You've blazed your own trail!"

"Isn't it crazy how Holly is a spitting image of my grandma?"

"She sure is."

"Holly has the same second-grade-teacher-nice-person mentality. She's warm, pure, a little naïve, a college cheerleader, and she loves to dance at halftimes of college basketball games and in the dance studios."

"I'll tell you what, though— this is not your grand-mother's kind of dance studio."

"I know. Dad, I look at it more of as an art gallery. Holly has even come in here with me with Josh, Alex and their girl-friends. Besides, what Grandma doesn't know won't hurt her."

"Perhaps," I laughed.

"Dad, do you want to shoot some pool?"

"Sure, as long as you don't whine when the old man kicks your ass."

As he laughed, the boy, who wasn't a boy anymore, led me toward an open table. A cute dancer approached. She ironically resembled Tyler's girlfriend, Holly, with below-the-shoulder light brown hair and an athletic figure. She was wearing a lacy white bra and matching thong with crystal pumps.

"Hi Tyler! How are you tonight?"

"I'm great. Paradise, I'd like you to meet my dad."

"I'm Billy," I said as I shook her hand.

"Nice to meet you, Billy. Your son is pretty amazing."

"I'd have to agree with you, Paradise. It's an honor to meet you."

"Ty, are you married or engaged yet?"

"Not yet!"

"If you ever get back on the market, you know where to find me."

We all laughed in unison.

While finishing the first and then a second pitcher, I let the boy win the best-of-seven series in pool, 4-3.

"Nice effort Dad," he said. "The beer tab's now on you."

"When isn't the beer tab on me?"

"Shall we eat? Can't beat the $5 Steak Special."

"Sure, Son. Works for me."

"Let's get a table."

As we walked back toward the dining tables, another dancer approached us. This one was a chesty, leggy blonde with hair extensions running down to the top of her backside.

"Hey Ty!" she said as her eyes lit up and she wrapped her arms around my son in a tight embrace.

After they released the embrace, Tyler turned to introduce us.

"Dad, this is Ayla. Ayla, my dad, Billy."

"Ayla as in *Clan of the Cave Bear*?"

"Yes. My real name is Jean after the author, Jean Auel. *Clan of the Cave Bear* is one of my favorite novels as well as my mother's."

"Wow, Jean… errr… Ayla, I mean. She has always been one of my favorites. That's a great name."

"Your boy here is one of my heroes, Billy."

"Really, I can't say I'm surprised. He's also one of mine. He does seem to know a lot of the girls here."

"Well, he's a regular and he tips extremely well, but most importantly, I love him for his manners, charisma, and hygiene."

"I'm not surprised, Ayla. Good to know about the hygiene."

"Yeah, and it's obvious he gets his manners and charisma from his dad," Ayla said as she winked and walked away.

After a delicious steak dinner, complete with salad and fries and our third pitcher of Bud Light, the conversation came full circle.

"Anyway, Dad, where were we on the phone, earlier today?"

"Son, I believe you were saying that I was a horrible father."

"I think you are a horrible father."

"I'm sorry you feel that way. But can we talk about the boy?"

"Trystan?"

"Yeah. Son, your nephew, your sister, FAITH's son. Your dad's grandson. Tyler, did you skip kindergarten? Did your sisters skip kindergarten? Then why did your mom have the kid skip kindergarten?"

"She said it wasn't her decision. She said that the principal claims it's Oregon state law that all kids who are six must be put in first grade."

"He just turned six. Son, I hate to tell you this for the thousandth time, but your mother is full of shit."

"Don't get started going off on my mom again, Dad. You need to stop text-harassing her or you're going to get thrown in jail."

"Text-harassing her? You mean like the one I sent the first week of school?"

Grandma Diane!
Why is Trystan skipping kindergarten? Please do not interpret this message as my harassing you. I love my grandson and if you stand around and allow this to happen, then I question your concern for him. He should NOT be put in first grade. If you do this, for the rest of Trystan's life, there will be HELL to pay.

Education is not to be taken lightly. He's not ready for first grade, and you are setting him up for failure. This is not something to be stubborn about or fool around with. I'm not being angry here, just passionate about my grandson's future. First grade is not a daycare center. If you want to discuss this, feel free to call.

Did Tyler or our girls skip kindergarten? THINK! Really THINK about this...

Thanks, Billy

"Dad, that's harassment in my book."

"Son, you have a right to your opinion. I think it's more of a wake-up call! Also, there's no such law that your mom was referring to earlier. She's putting words in the principal's mouth."

"Listen, Dad, I've got a nice life and you have a way of trying to ruin it. I just want you to leave me alone from now on. I now know what you did and I am SICK over it."

"What did I do, Son?"

"You slept with my sister!"

"Huh?

"That's what makes you a terrible father."

"Jesus, Son, where is this coming from? Is that what your mom is telling you?"

"No, she doesn't even know. I haven't told her because it's too shameful. Faith told me herself."

"Huh?"

"Faith told me that you got her blackout drunk and then dragged her up your stairs and had sex with her."

I slid my chair back and raised my hands above my head, interlocking my fingers while taking a deep breath.

"Son, you don't believe this. You wouldn't have agreed to have a beer and play pool if you truly believed this happened."

"Dad, in my book I'd call you a *Sick Fuck* if that happened!"

"Son, it's very crushing to even hear you say that, but rest assured I've never slept with *either* of your sisters."

"Okay, I'll take your word, but why did you pimp Faith out?"

"Son, what do you mean?"

"How much money did you make off the tabloid stories?"

"Now we're getting somewhere. Son, why do you even care? Why are you talking for your mom, again?"

"Dad, I want to know."

"I don't mind telling you, Son, but I just want to know why you're slinging arrows all over the place. All I did was try to explain to you why I thought it wasn't a good idea for you to hire your mom."

"I'm over that, Dad. I let that go months ago."

"Well good. Now, if you must know, most of the money went to pay off the back alimony the state said I owed your mom. You and I have talked countless times about the reasons why I did not owe it to her and how I've been more than generous to her. I think I've done enough, Son. I'm finished with her."

"Then, Dad, why are you still in love with Mom?"

"Tyler, are you back to smoking pot again?"

"No, Dad, I gave that up long ago. Besides, my company does random drug testing all the time and it's just not worth the risk."

"So you've outgrown it?"

"Yeah, Dad. So are you telling me you can move on with your life, without Mom?"

"I'm sorry to tell you this, but your mom and I will never get back together. We just weren't meant to be."

"But you seem obsessed with Mom, if you ask me."

"Son, I am not stalking your mom."

"Well, she says you fit all the descriptions."

"She's entitled to her opinions, misguided as they are."

"And you're sure you didn't sleep with my sister?"

"Son, I hate to tell you this. But you're getting your sister's story mixed up with your mother's."

"What do you mean?"

"For years, I tried to get your mom to work through her problems. Now, you're in your twenties so I guess you're ready to handle the truth. Your mom's dad and stepbrother… Yes, your Grandpa Henry and Uncle Daniel molested your mom when she was a kid. It started when she was as far back as age five and ran well into her teens."

"DAD, don't be bullshitting me!"

"Son, I'm sorry. People can't get better if they don't want to face their fears and talk their way through psychoanalysis, with skilled psychiatrists or psychologists. Your mom was the one who used to get drunk when she was a kid. She'd black out, and her dad and stepbrother did terrible things to her."

"I can't believe it, Dad. But what about the stairs? Their house didn't have two stories."

"I don't know about the stairs. Maybe they were in your mom's nightmares or at a relative's home. It took her years to finally tell me. But I could never help convince her to get therapy. Many of her friends knew it was going on, but she asked them to keep quiet."

"Friends? Who are they?"

"Mary, Chris and Ginger for starters. I've talked to them about it and they've confirmed."

"I'm going to knock the shit out of Grandpa Henry and Uncle Daniel!"

"Son, that won't do you any good. You know where that'll get you."

"I know, I know…Measure 11, assault, and a mandatory jail sentence."

"Yeah, they're not worth going to jail for seventy months."

"No shit, Dad."

"Now, Son, we need to get Trystan into kindergarten. Will you tell your mom and Erasmo to get this done right away?"

"I'll mention it. But it's not my decision. Erasmo is the dad."

"Yeah, Son, but he'll listen to you."

"I'll see what I can do. In the meantime, Faith needs rehab so Trystan is better off with Mom and Erasmo until Faith gets better."

"I agree. Your sister needs rehab. She's found a facility in Eugene that allows mothers to recover while living with their kids. Will you support her being in a place like that?"

"I'm not sure."

"Now you're starting to sound like your mom. Is she still drinking?"

"Dad, she's been sober for five years."

"You're sure?"

"Yeah, that's what she tells me. Dad, it's getting late. Thanks for shooting pool, the beer, and the dinner. I gotta go."

"You're welcome. Let's do it again sometime. Son, here are a couple twenties. Be sure to tip Paradise and Ayla for us!"

"Will do."

As I was leaving George's Dancin' Bare, I got a phone call from Faith. She had entered a year-long residential alcohol treatment program at a facility called Anna's House, in the country just southwest of Eugene. Believe it or not, her mother had recommended the Christian-based rehab center.

"Dad, there's something I need to tell you. I recently found out that the divorce papers Mom helped me file in 2006 were never finalized."

"Jesus, Faith! So you mean to tell me that you're still legally married?"

"*Technically*, I am. Dad, but wait! The good news is that I got an attorney two months ago. His name is David Devine. David drew up new papers and then a month ago, my friend Sandy served Erasmo again at the McDonald's in Central Point."

"So, you were waiting for the month to transpire before you told me?"

"Exactly. Dad, we haven't been together for four years."

"Let's go down to Southern Oregon and get this taken care of."

"Okay, Dad."

"I'll pick you up in the morning."

"Dad, there's one catch."

"What's that?"

"The last time I was down there, I left my suitcase at Mom's and the final papers are in there. If she knows that I'll get full custody of Trystan, then she probably won't let me have those papers."

"We'll just have to see what we can do. If she doesn't give them to you, we'll just have to get some new ones."

After staying the night at a motel in Medford, the next day we attempted to visit Trystan at Oak Grove Elementary School. It was obvious Diane had put the office staff on alert. We entered the building, approached the main office, and Faith introduced herself at the main window. At least three of the ladies scurried around and dashed into the principal's office.

A rather large, stereotypical female administrator-looking lady approached us.

"Hello, I'm Principal Julie Evans."

"Hi, I'm Faith Freeman. I'm Trystan Ayala-Freeman's mother. This is my dad, Trystan's grandpa, Bill. We're here to see my son."

"Oh, I'd love to let you see Trystan, but he's absent today."

"Absent?" I said. "How's his attendance been this year?"

"Actually…it's been perfect…that is…until today."

"Okay. Thank you," I continued. "Do you have five minutes we could talk to you about his grade placement and his progress?"

"Oh, I'm so sorry. I'm swamped. Today's just not good. I'll need for you to make an appointment through my office assistant. I should be able to see you Friday after school."

Damn, I thought. Today's Tuesday. I want to get the hell out of here tonight, if possible.

Faith's eyes started to water up.

"It's okay," I said. "We've come all the way down from Portland and Eugene. We're probably not going to be here through Friday. But we'll call if we decide that will work."

I put my arm around Faith and led her outside back to the car. Her tears were starting to flow.

"Dad, they're trying to keep my son from me. It's just not fair."

I blew out a deep breath. "Okay, we just move onto the next issue at hand. Let's go get your suitcase from your mom."

We drove from Medford to Ashland. It was a beautiful Indian summer afternoon in Southern Oregon. The temps were in the upper seventies. I did not come down here for a confrontation so I decided to play it safe and drop my daughter off three blocks down the street from her mom's apartment.

"Where are you going, Dad?"

"I'm heading over to Hunter Park, throw a blanket down under a shady tree and read my novel. I'll only be a few minutes away."

"What are you reading, now?"

"It's Grisham… *An Innocent Man.*"

"*An Innocent Man*? I like the title."

"Yeah. It's a good book about a high school baseball star who becomes a man wrongly accused. Anyway, call me after you have the suitcase and I'll pick you up right here."

"Will do, Dad. Hopefully Mom will be coming home from work soon and we won't have to be here all night."

"Just think of it as a stakeout. You've got your phone, huh?"

"Yeah."

I made my way to Hunter Park. As I placed the blanket down in the shade, I looked at the two Little League baseball/softball fields and reminisced about what seemed like simpler times when I coached my three kids and the biggest controversy of life was brought on by opposing coaches who wanted to enforce a "no-bubble-gum" rule. I'd loaded up my kids and their teammates with wads of Bubble Yum while protesting the other so-called "adult's" crusade to enforce a "safety" rule. I saw it as a military-style attempt to prevent kids from being kids.

"Bubble gum with Little League baseball is a God-given right," I said as I stated my case to the high-school-aged umpiring crew.

"What are you going to do when one of your kids chokes?" asked the opposing coach.

"The Heimlich maneuver, of course."

"You're breaking the rules."

"No, my kids are just getting in your head. There is no such rule."

My kids won that game against the best team in town. Funny thing, though, the next time we played them, every one of the other team's kids was chewing bubble gum and the outcome for us wasn't as fortunate.

I'd been cruising into the Grisham story for nearly two hours when I felt my phone vibrate. It was Faith, and she was sending text messages and text photos.

Jesus, I thought. Diane has fallen off the wagon again. And why am I not surprised? The photos showed two, clear garbage bags loaded with empty bottles of Coors Light, Diane's favorite. Also, inside one of her two cars was an open container—a half-consumed bottle of Carlo Rossi wine, underneath a sweatshirt on the floor of the passenger seat. In the back was Trystan's car seat, which Diane had borrowed from Faith.

Shortly thereafter, my phone started to ring. It wasn't Faith's number but rather a local Ashland land line.

"Hello."

"Dad, my phone battery is drained."

"Where are you?"

"I'm at the paint store. They let me use their phone. Get this, I just saw a cop drive down the street toward Mom's."

"No shit? I'll be right there. We need to show the cop the opened container."

I flew to my feet, grabbed up the blanket and novel and zipped into my car. Within minutes, Faith was in the car and we dashed towards the apartment complex on McGill Drive.

"Faith, why do you think the cop's heading to your mom's?"

"I don't know. Maybe a neighbor saw me sitting on her stairs and taking pictures of inside her car."

As we turned the corner, to our surprise, there was no cop car but rather Faith's mother.

"Jesus, Faith, get the suitcase and if she's got Trystan, I'll grab him and let's get the hell out of Dodge."

The next few minutes zipped by in slow motion. Diane's new Pontiac Solstice sports car was parked behind her old Chevy Cavalier, the car with the opened bottle of wine and the grandson's car seat. I pulled behind her car as Faith snapped a couple photos of the new car.

Diane ran up the stairs of her apartment complex, opened her front door, then dashed back to the Pontiac. She reached in and grabbed her phone and her garage door opener, and then darted over to close her garage door. There was no sign of the boy.

"I'm here to get my suitcase, Mom."

"Oh, I think it's in the front room. Come up and get it."

"Di, where's the kid?"

She ignored me as she led Faith into her apartment. Within two seconds Faith came back out.

"GET OUT OF MY HOUSE!" yelled Diane.

"Mom, I just want my suitcase."

"I DON'T HAVE IT. YOUR SISTER HAS IT IN PORT-LAND!"

"Faith, let's go," I said.

Knowing Diane, it would be only a matter of moments before she'd be calling 9-1-1. I was not there to have any more of my time wasted. I had already started to back out when Faith opened her door. By that time, Diane already had Ashland P.D. on the phone. I could hear her as she shouted into her phone: "OFFICER! MY EX-HUSBAND IS STALKING ME! HE'S HERE AT MY HOME AND HE SAID HE'S GOING TO RUN ME OVER WITH HIS CAR!"

As Faith sat down, she attempted to close the door but her mom twisted and threw her larger-than-life backside into the car, practically landing on Faith's lap.

"MOM!" Faith laughed. "Let me close the door."

Diane continued her tirade on her "emergency" call!

"OFFICER! My daughter is BI-POLAR! SHE NEEDS A MENTAL EVALUATION!"

"Mom, have you been drinking already? Dad, don't you smell it?"

"Damn, come to think of it, I smell alcohol, but I also smell pot."

By that time Diane had released herself and moved away from the car as Faith was able to shut her door.

"Diane, you'd better not be drinking and driving with the kid in your car!"

"OFFICER, MY EX-HUSBAND AND MY DAUGHTER ARE CROSSING MY BOUNDARIES!"

"Mom, are you relapsing?" Faith asked.

"RELAPSING IS PART OF RECOVERY!"

"Mom, you're sounding paranoid."

"I'M NOT PARANOID!"

Faith and I just looked and shrugged at each other as I started to pull away.

"THAT POT SMELL IS FROM MY OFFICE! WE HAVE MEDICAL MARIJUANA PATIENTS! They are perfectly legal."

After heading north on I-5 for about ten minutes, I decided to pull over to the side of the freeway and make a 9-1-1 phone call of my own.

"This is 9-1-1 dispatch."

"I'd like to report an intoxicated 5150 in Ashland at 2812 McGill Drive. Her name is Diane Christine Downer. She might be driving my six-year-old grandson around, and I want a police officer sent over there to assure the boy's safety."

"Sir, did you say, 5150?"

"I did."

"What do mean?"

"5150 is the police code number for a person needing to be committed to a psych ward for being either a danger to herself and/or others around her."

"I did know that. It's the code in California but we don't use numbers in Oregon."

"Then what do you use?"

"We call it *Plain Talk*."

"Plain Talk?"

"Yes. Someone who needs a legal voluntary psychiatric hold is an A.M.I.P or an Allegedly Mentally Ill Person."

"That works for me. Call her whatever you want, but all I know is she's been drinking again and she's losing it."

"I'll get a police officer right over there. Oh, and come to think of it, wasn't *5150* a Van Halen album?"

"The first one Sammy ever sang on...and you know something else?"

"What's that?"

"You can tell the officer you're dispatching that if he needs something to confirm Downer's identity, unless she's had it removed, she's got a tramp stamp with the number '5150' above an infinity symbol."

"Really? That sounds creative."

"Yeah. *5150* is one of my favorite albums, as is Journey's *Infinity*."

After giving the dispatcher my contact info, I shot Diane a (text) message of my own...

Attention Diane: Regarding OUR daughter and YOUR bound-aries...

It must really make you feel outstanding that so many beautiful, classy, conscientious women can see through all the CRAP you're trying to pull on Faith, and they are picking up YOUR slack by being there for her. I'm bewildered while Faith's own mother, an alleged "rehabilitated" alcoholic, continues refusing to care or help her in any way. Do you realize how many people bent over backwards so you could go on your 2005 five-week rehabilitation vacation only to have "Husband #2" piss away 15k so you could bang fellow inmates in Idaho?!!! Did you ever thank anybody for helping you with that?

Thank god for Megan, and dozens of others... It's a shame that they are doing your job! You still are an embarrassment and a sorry excuse for a mother. This is a wakeup call! You're almost 50 for chrissakes! Drive to Bend and once and for all ask Henry why he molested you?!!! I'm tired of being your goddamn scapegoat! Why haven't you ever told OUR son, Tyler, that your dad, Henry, is the "Sick Fuck" and NOT his own dad? Tyler probably wouldn't call his dad that if you finally stepped up and behaved like a mom and finally made things right! I'm sorry to be harsh but the way you've never treated your kids as equals has never been fair to any of them.

Let me know when you're ready to sit down and discuss things so everyone can start to heal and go forward. I want you to have a relationship with Faith and Trystan... for a lifetime... but unless you try to mend fences immediately, your days are numbered.

~ Billy... (the father of your children)

CHAPTER 4:

Stalking the Grandson

The next morning, while I was squeezing in a quick five-mile run around Medford, Faith printed the divorce paperwork off the Internet at the motel office. Then she called the school to check on Trystan's attendance.

"Mom and Erasmo kept him out of school again, Dad," she said as her voice began to crack. "Dad, this just isn't fair. They won't even let me see my son."

"I know how you're being treated is not right. But we have to stay the course. Let's get to the courthouse and see if we can shake anything loose over there."

After going through the metal detectors, we approached a lady at the window. Her nameplate said "Barbara".

"Hi Barbara, this is my daughter Faith. We're concerned about the status of her divorce. You see, her husband is an illegal alien, and a flight risk, and we're worried he might take her son, Trystan, at any moment and flee to Mexico."

Barbara began looking up the status on her computer.

"The father is Erasmo Ayala-Rangel?"

"Yes."

Barbara's eyes immediately lit up. "Listen, Erasmo defaulted on challenging the divorce by not replying in thirty days."

"Do you have the final divorce docs?"

"Yes, right here."

"There's a table over to my left. Go over there, sit down, fill out and sign the papers. If you get them back to me in the next thirty minutes, I'll get them up to Judge Thomas and you should be divorced by the end of today."

Faith quickly dashed over to the table, pulled out a pen and zipped through the forms.

"Dad, it's asking me what do I believe he owes me for support? What should I put down?"

"What do you think?"

"Erasmo always says since he's illegal, nobody will ever be able to make him pay me."

"Put down three hundred dollars a month. At least that's something."

"I'm just going to leave it blank. I don't care if I get support or not. I just want to escape and be free."

After Faith gave the finished forms to Barbara, we decided to get a bite to eat. We went to the Asian Grill for the yellow curry with chicken, veggies, and a side of peanut sauce. After lunch, the waiting game continued. We decided to go for a walk through the Rogue Valley Mall. At 3:30, Faith got a phone call. It was Barbara.

"Yes," said Faith. "Okay, uh huh… then go ahead with three hundred. Thank you, so much Barbara. Uh huh, we're on our way over."

"So what's up?" I asked.

"Barbara said that Judge Thomas would sign off on it only if I took child support."

"So?"

"I went with three hundred a month. Dad, if we get over there now, he might sign off of it today!"

We took a seat in the lobby at four. At 4:45, Barbara waved us over.

"Congratulations! You are divorced! Here's a certified copy of the decree."

Faith had been granted full custody of her son, Trystan, by Jackson County Circuit Court Judge Arthur Thomas.

"YESSS!" Faith shouted. "Dad, thank you."

"It was a team effort," I replied as my daughter reached out and gave me a big bear hug!

"Now what, Dad?"

"What do you mean?"

"Mom and Erasmo are still hiding him from us."

"We're going to drive over to your mom's and you're going to show her the judge's order. Then we're going to get your kid and escape from this hell hole!"

After dropping Faith off three blocks away for the second day in a row, neither Faith nor I should have been surprised this time that Diane was not home. Not only was she not there, Diane had wised up and did not appear after work. By nine o'clock that night, we agreed that we would call it an evening and then try again in the morning. I sent Faith a text a bit earlier asking her to rendezvous again at the paint store. She called shortly thereafter.

"Mom must be staying at her boyfriend's or somewhere else," said Faith.

"She can't keep doing this."

"Dad, don't you need to get back to your job? Maybe you should leave me with friends and I'll stay until I get my boy."

"Faith, I appreciate that but I'm not leaving until we get Trystan. They can't hide him forever."

"Thanks Dad. You're my hero."

"Thanks Faith. We're in this together. Now meet me at the paint store."

"I will, Dad, but I just noticed that the light is on in Mom's garage and there are some small windows toward the top."

"Well, snap a couple photos and get over here."

A few minutes later, Faith came sprinting around the corner and leaped into the car!

"Dad, you're not going to believe it. Look at my phone."

"Jesus, Faith! She has your goddamn suitcase! I thought she said your sister had it?"

"She did say that, and Libby is in Portland. Mom is trying to sabotage my divorce! If I don't get divorced, she doesn't have to give me my kid. What a bitch!"

"Was her Chevy there with the wine bottle?"

"No, that car has disappeared."

"We could have figured on that one."

"Dad, what's our next move?"

"Tomorrow we're going into the DHS and show them your divorce papers and drill them until they make Erasmo and your mother bring the boy in."

At eight the next morning, Faith and I took a seat in the DHS lobby since the receptionist told us that none of the caseworkers had reported for work yet. Ten minutes later, Faith decided to call Oak Grove Elementary School.

"Hi this is Faith Freeman. I was wondering if my son, Trystan, is in attendance."

This time, Faith's eyes lit up as she pulled on my arm and headed for the door.

"Dad, let's go! He's in school!"

We rocketed the three miles across Medford.

"Okay, Faith. You've got to be cool. Make sure you've got those divorce papers and realize they'll probably pose some resistance."

I parked the car and then Faith and I entered the building.

"Hello again," Faith said to the receptionist at the front desk. "I'm here to have my son released."

"The grandmother said you have no rights to the grandson!"

I couldn't help myself going with the *Wayne's World* classic query line.

"A sphincter says what?"

"Dad, this is serious," Faith said as she pulled out the divorce papers from her purse, and handed them out to the receptionist.

"Judge Thomas granted me full custody of my son yesterday. Here's a certified copy of his order to verify the judgment."

The receptionist approached, briefly looked them over before replying, "May I make a copy of these documents? Then I'll get these documents right to Principal Evans."

"Thank you," Faith replied.

A few moments later, Principal Evans came out of her office.

"Good morning."

"Good morning, Principal Evans," Faith and I said in unison.

"Would you like to come back to my office?"

I touched Faith on the arm. "But we don't have an appointment, and it's only Thursday."

"Oh, that's okay,"

"On Tuesday, didn't you say if the boy was in attendance, you'd let us see him?"

"I did," she replied.

"Well, isn't he here today?"

"He is. But DHS is sending personnel over and now they want to discuss this matter."

"Okay then, yes, we'd like to talk to you in your office."

Principal Evans led us back to her office. There were two seats positioned directly across from her desk. A framed photo of her, with who appeared to be her husband and two boys, was positioned on one side of her desk.

"Thank you for sitting down with us, Principal Evans," I said.

"That's my job."

"What we wanted to discuss earlier this week was the grandson's grade placement. Why was Trystan placed into first grade when he attended preschool last year?"

"Wasn't he six years old when school began, Mr. Freeman?"

"He was."

"Well, our district policy says that we place the student in first grade if he is age six prior to the start of the year."

"Principal Evans. What if the student is not ready?"

"Then we evaluate that on an individual basis."

"So if that's the case, then he could be assigned into kindergarten?"

"Yes, there are always exceptions."

"Principal Evans, are those your boys in this picture?"

"Yes."

"Did your boys skip kindergarten?"

"No, they didn't, Mr. Freeman."

"Well, neither did my boy, nor his sisters, and we'd prefer that Trystan not skip kindergarten either. Why did you allow this to happen?"

"Mr. Freeman, the grandmother and Trystan's father placed him in first grade."

"Let me ask you this. If the grandmother had requested that the grandson be placed in kindergarten, you could and would have made this happen?"

"Absolutely."

"And it's not a state law that the kid can't be in kindergarten?"

"Most definitely not!"

"Okay, the grandmother claims that the state law is keeping him out of kindergarten and so, we're now a month into school and this child has been inappropriately placed into the wrong grade."

"Yes, I see your point."

"Well, that's why we're here today. To take him to Eugene to live with his mother and place him in kindergarten."

Before responding, Principal Evans excused herself to answer her phone.

"The DHS workers are here. Shall we go meet with them? We can do it in the conference room."

As Principal Evans led us out of her office and across the hall, out of the main office window, I could see three Medford cop cars pull into the parking lot. Oh shit, I thought. The last thing we need is any of us getting arrested. Medford, and all other Oregon school districts, have been on high alert ever since the Kyron Horman kid from Portland had disappeared from school last spring. As a result, most school district personnel have had special abduction in-service training to prevent a repeat of the Kyron Horman ordeal, in which his stepmother dropped the seven-year-old off outside his classroom in June, only to have him vanish. Medford Public Schools are especially vigilant since Kyron's mother, Desiree Young, lives in Medford.

As we entered the conference room, two portly ladies sat at the table with a male Medford police officer. Principal Evans started the intros.

"I'm Julie Evans, principal here at Oak Grove."

"This is Becky Mosier, I'm Lynda Hall, Trystan's DHS caseworker, and this is Officer Mike Jackson."

Faith shook all of their hands and introduced herself. I did the same and added, "I'm the grandfather."

Faith produced the certified divorce papers signed by Judge Thomas and explained that she had entered into a residential treatment facility in Eugene. Ms. Mosier and Ms. Hall expressed their concern for the "overall well-being of the child" and wanted to be assured that the rehab facility in Eugene was legit and that there were safe accommodations for the grandson. Faith produced a business card for the Anna's House treatment center and gave it to Lynda and Becky, who left the room to call their supervisor and make the calls to check on the Eugene center. Officer Jackson waited with us. About twenty minutes later, the pair returned.

"All right, we've talked to all of those involved and we are going to allow you to take your son with you to Eugene. The police are escorting Trystan down here from his classroom as we speak. We will be transferring your case to the Lane County DHS."

Faith broke down in tears.

"Thank you, thank you, thank you!" she said.

About five minutes later, Principal Evans opened the conference room door and the little guy appeared. He looked good, healthy, and happy. This was the first time I'd seen him in three months. Faith hadn't seen him in a month.

He dashed over and hugged Faith.

"Hi Momma. Where's my grandma?" he asked.

"I'm sure she's at work, buddy," said Faith.

"I want my grandma."

"You'll see her again, someday."

We nodded a thank you to everybody. The three Medford cops walked with us out to the school parking lot.

Within thirty minutes we were finally out of Jackson County. The boy was free. He had escaped. By the time we reached Eugene, Faith received a call from Becky. She put the phone on speaker.

"Your mom stormed into our office only a few minutes after we had returned from meeting with you."

"Becky, I'm not surprised. What did she say?"

"She screamed, 'MY DAUGHTER IS A TERRIBLE MOTHER! YOU PROMISED ME THAT YOU WOULD NOT LET MY GRANDSON LEAVE WITH THEM! YOU PROMISED ME YOU WOULDN'T LET THEM TAKE HIM. YOU PROMISED. SHE IS A BI-POLAR. SHE IS A TERRIBLE MOTHERRRRRRR!'"

CHAPTER 5:

Temporary Stalking Order

Two weeks had transpired since Trystan had broken free of his grandmother. He had settled into his new kindergarten class in Eugene, getting extra reading and math help. Since then he had made noticeable and remarkable academic progress. Faith was also able to register him for youth soccer and basketball, even though the seasons had already begun. Most importantly, Faith had provided a stable routine in Trystan's life. Her own life was becoming more stable as well. She was continuing her healing and recovery process. I decided to take a sabbatical from financial advising to pursue my freelance writing career and to focus more on my triathlon training.

We later would find out that during this time Diane was in the face of the Jackson County DHS caseworkers on a daily basis. She was tearing Faith's parental reputation apart and demanding they bring the grandson back to Southern Oregon. I have to admit, ill-advised as it usually is, Diane's tenacity is commendable.

A "shelter hearing" had been scheduled for mid-October. According to the DHS workers in Medford, it would be the final court gathering before they would transfer Trystan's case to Lane County. The purpose of the hearing was simply to assure that Trystan had a safe place to sleep, was being fed, and was enrolled in school. Faith would be allowed to attend the hearing by phone.

Immediately after the hearing, Faith called me in hysterics.

"DAD! Mom blindsided me! She and Erasmo told the judge that you had committed perjury on the divorce papers."

"Huh? Faith, Hold on... take some deep breaths and calm down."

"CALM DOWN? Mom is on her way up here with Erasmo to take Trystan back to Medford!"

"What? I thought this was just a 'shelter hearing'?"

"They told the judge that Erasmo was never served and you forged his signature on the papers."

"Faith, you know I didn't sign his name on the papers. And your friend Sandy served him."

"We know that but he's playing the *Poor-dumb-Mexican* card and the *I-don't-understand-English-so-I-was-never-served* card."

"So who was the judge and what did the judge say?"

"It was Judge Sorro. She said that she was rescinding Judge Thomas' decision and putting it on hold until Erasmo and I go through mediation and determine custody."

"Jesus, Judge Thomas already determined custody."

"Did you tell Judge Sorro that Erasmo is an illegal alien?"

"Yeah, and she said that it's juvenile court and it's not for her to rule on that issue."

"No shit? Wow."

"Dad, they said that she's putting Trystan back in DHS custody and they're giving him to the father since I haven't finished rehab."

"Faith, I don't know what to say. I need to collect my thoughts."

"And get this, Dad. Mom told me years ago to go to Anna's House since it was 'Christian-based' rehab. I came here because of her. Today in court she pleaded that it isn't an Oregon-State sponsored facility so it wasn't a valid center. The judge asked the Anna's House director this question over the phone and apparently Judge Sorro didn't like the director's answer because all the judge did was laugh at her. The courthouse was full of Erasmo's illegal Mexican buddies and family and we didn't stand a chance!"

"Shitphuc. Do you want me to run down there and pick you up? We could make a break for Idaho."

"No. Then you'd get in trouble, Dad. But what should I do?"

"What's next on the court schedule with DHS?"

"They're going to have a custody and visitation review hearing in four weeks on November 18."

"Maybe you should enroll in a state-certified rehab program like Serenity Lane?"

"That's what I'm thinking, Dad."

"You can probably bust through the program there in three weeks and be done by November 18."

Sure enough, 15,000 bucks and three weeks later, Faith had successfully completed her state-certified treatment program at Serenity Lane in Eugene. If it weren't for that Matthew Fox story, Faith would have had a hard time affording the treatment. She was required to continue with outpatient care and AA meetings. Faith dutifully followed the court's instructions.

During this time, I ran Internet background checks on both Diane and Erasmo. I wasn't shocked to find that both of them had received DUI citations within the last year.

"Faith, correct me if I'm wrong but if we asked your brother or sister how long your mom has been sober, what would they say?"

"You know, Tyler's told both of us that Mom's been sober for five years, since he and I did the intervention on her in fall 2005. I'm sure that's what Libby believes as well."

"Okay, I sure hope Erasmo isn't driving. Did you know that he doesn't have a valid license and he's using a social security number which belongs to a woman named Sara Enegren, from Wichita, Kansas?"

"Dad, are you sure? How'd you find all that out?"

"I did my homework and paid thirty-five bucks to a private-eye website. Next time you get a chance, you should ask your mom how long she's been sober."

Also, while Faith was in rehab, I received some telephone calls from Officer Vaughn Seward, an Ashland Police Officer. Officer Seward and I played phone tag before we finally connected, a couple days before the DHS custody/visitation hearing.

"Mr. Freeman, this is Vaughn Seward, Ashland P.D."

"Hi, Officer Seward. Let me tell you right now, up front, if your contacting me has anything to do about my ex-wife Diane calling the cops back in September, she's a relapsed alcoholic and anytime you interact with her, she needs to be breathalyzered and drug tested."

"Mr. Freeman, it doesn't matter whether she's intoxicated or not when I talk to her. She doesn't want you talking to her, she doesn't want you calling her, she doesn't want you texting her, and she doesn't want you e-mailing her. She doesn't want you coming to her house so it doesn't matter if she's intoxicated or not. She doesn't want those things."

"Okay, Officer Seward, I hear where you're coming from. So if someone is drunk or stoned, their words are to be taken with the same respect as those who are sober?"

"Your ex-wife could be a prostitute, a predator, or suicidal. She could have put poison in your food, sold drugs with your son, told your kids you did things to them when they were too young to remember. If she doesn't want you to contact her, then you aren't allowed to by the law."

"Vaughn, did she tell you that I haven't seen her in fifteen months and she tried to play the harassment card in Portland a year ago and it was thrown out by a judge?"

"No, she didn't."

"Has she told you that she got a DUI in Medford on Highway 99 at three a.m. on November 14, 2009, yet somehow she's still been sober for five years?"

"No, she has not."

"Has she told you that I'm obsessed with her, still in love with her, and I am stalking her?"

"As a matter of fact, she did tell me all of those things."

"And you believed her?"

"She hasn't given me a reason not to."

"Am I giving you any reasons not to believe her?"

"It's not my job to make judgments. That's for the courts."

"Vaughn, I don't mean any disrespect, but do you have any outside contact or interest in my ex-wife?"

"Outside contact?"

"Yeah, like away from work."

"I don't see what the relevance is here."

"Vaughn, do you have kids?"

"I do."

"Did any of your kids skip kindergarten?"

"No, but I'm still not getting your point, Mr. Freeman."

"The only incidences when I've contacted her in the last year have been for two reasons. First, our daughter was put in the hospital last summer. Second, after Diane assumed custody of our grandson, she mistakenly requested that the kid skip kindergarten and be placed into the first grade, where he's now suffering and failing. I love my grandson and I'm not going to keep quiet over this issue."

"I see, Mr. Freeman."

"Does this mean I'm stalking her, Vaughn?"

"Mr. Freeman, for your edification, Diane Downer did not appear intoxicated nor did she smell intoxicated when I spoke with her."

"Vaughn, I don't want any trouble. Now, I haven't contacted her in weeks. I need to come down there on the eighteenth for the DHS custody and visitation hearing. I'm hoping for a peaceful, productive experience for the kid's sake. Besides fixing his grade placement in school, I simply want to make sure that his grandmother is not driving drunk while he's in her car. Is that too much to ask?"

"Not at all, Mr. Freeman."

"Thanks, Vaughn, now I've got to run. Oh, there is one more thing. I've received at least seven e-mails from Di in the last two months. Isn't it odd for someone who doesn't want contact to be sending e-mails to her alleged stalker?"

"I'd have to agree with you on that one, Mr. Freeman."

"Could I forward the e-mails to you? So when you call her back to tell her we talked could you ask her about them?"

"Will do, and I'll call you back to let you know what I find out."

My parents joined Faith and me in the Jackson County Juvenile Courthouse lobby about fifteen minutes prior to Trystan's child custody/visitation hearing. Tyler, Libby, Erasmo and Diane were seated on a bench, but they immediately headed to the courtroom when they saw us approaching. Within five minutes I noticed an Ashland cop come through the doorway and directly toward me. I assumed it was Vaughn Seward so I stood up and approached him.

"Are you Billy Freeman?"

"I am. Are you Vaughn Seward?"

"I'm not. He had to attend to another matter so I came in his place."

"Well, I'm sorry to tell you this, but I'm not talking to you. I'm only talking to Vaughn."

"Mr. Freeman, I have some papers to serrr…"

I immediately dashed to the door. I shouted, "I AM UNABLE TO HEAR YOU. AND I WON'T BE TALKING TO ANYBODY UNTIL I SPEAK TO AN ATTORNEY."

I made it safely outside, then I turned to the right and walked two blocks down the street. I started to call Kivel and Howard, the Portland law firm which has represented me with a number of legal issues in the past. When I saw the Ashland "stalker cop" turn to the left, walking away leaving the scene, I decided not to make the call. I noticed my dad had just walked outside, picking up a piece of piece of litter off the ground. He threw the litter into a nearby trash can.

I walked back toward the court building.

Judge Felicia Heron presided over this morning's proceedings, which were scheduled to review the grandson's current situation regarding living arrangements, visitation, and education.

Although my parents sat on the right side of the court room near Erasmo, Tyler, Libby and Diane, I chose to sit up front on the left side, directly behind Faith. I noticed Erasmo had a court-appointed interpreter.

The first person to speak was Tanny Flowers, who had now taken over the DHS case from Lynda Hall. Judge Heron asked Mr. Flowers if he could describe his observations including Trystan's current living situation and anything pertinent to his progress in school.

"Your Honor, Trystan is a very well-mannered, kind-natured, good six-year-old kid. He's currently living with his father, Erasmo, while his mother, Faith, completes a state-certified inpatient and outpatient alcohol treatment program. I've observed Trystan interacting with each of his parents on an individual basis and while I've been in the presence of both parents. It's evident that he receives a lot of love from not only his parents but also his additional family members. Many are in the room today. I've also observed him in his first-grade classroom at Oak Grove Elementary. Socially, he is performing well. He's made many friends, he plays on the playground with those friends and many of the kids include Trystan in their social circle in the cafeteria at lunch time. Academically, Trystan works hard to participate, he's not afraid to raise his hand to ask a question, but his teacher indicates following a recent testing period that Trystan is academically behind and he's struggling to perform at the first-grade level. Retaking the first grade might be a recommendation for next year."

After Mr. Flowers finished, Judge Heron asked if anybody in the court room would like to say anything.

My mom, Trystan's great-grandmother, stood up immediately.

"I would, Your Honor."

"Please state your name and your relationship to the child."

"I'm Mrs. Anita Freeman, Trystan's great-grandmother."

"Proceed, Mrs. Freeman."

"Your Honor, I am a retired elementary school teacher. I was a kindergarten and first grade teacher for more than twenty years in Oregon public schools in Salem, Bend, and eastern Oregon. Trystan has a late birthday for first grade and he simply was not ready and he should not have been allowed to skip kindergarten. I believe a grave disservice is being done to him and he should be immediately placed back into an appropriate kindergarten classroom, rather than make him retake the first grade again next year."

"Mrs. Freeman, how long have you been retired?" asked Judge Heron.

"Since 1996."

"So, more than ten years?"

"Yes, Your Honor, fourteen to be exact."

"Well, this is an interesting situation to say the least. I was just speaking to a friend of mine about this the other night at dinner and apparently it's more common these days for kids to retake first grade than maybe it was back during the time period which you taught."

"Your Honor, I would respectfully disagree. Kids, even those at Trystan's age, are smart. They know what's going on and if he isn't moved back now, he's missing out on learning essential skills which would prepare him for first grade, but he will have to live with the stigma of failing the first grade the rest of his life."

"We can agree to disagree, Mrs. Freeman. Do you have anything else to say?"

"Not at this time, Your Honor."

I waited to see if anybody else was going to stand. Since no one did, I was on.

"Please state you name, and relationship to the child."

"I'm William B. Freeman. I'm the grandfather."

"Proceed, Mr. Freeman."

"Thank you, Your Honor. I'd like to start by stating that I've been an educator in Oregon for more than twenty years as well. I've taught high school English and journalism in Oregon for six years and worked with high school journalism and publications students as a yearbook representative for Jostens Publishing Company. I recently earned a Master's in educational leadership from the University of Oregon and I'm considering becoming a school administrator. So I think that I'm as qualified of a professional as anybody in this room when it comes to education. I would say that my mother is dead-on with her comments about how my grandson is going to be stigmatized the remainder of his life if something is not done immediately. First, I'd really like to know why the grandmother and Erasmo were allowed to make the decision of allowing Trystan to skip kindergarten."

Erasmo slumped in his chair, played dumb and simply mustered a shrug while his interpreter rattled off my statements in Spanish.

"Is the grandmother in the courtroom?" asked Judge Heron.

Diane slowly and timidly raised her hand.

"Would you like to answer Mr. Freeman's question?"

Amazingly, Diane stood.

"Your Honor, we did not have a choice. The principal made the placement and she told us that there's a district policy and a state law saying six-year-olds must go into the first grade."

"Your Honor, Ms. Downer doesn't know what she's talking about. Our own son, Tyler, was six years old when he started kindergarten. There might be a 'recommended' district policy, but it's not mandatory and there is no state law, which she's referring to. Principal Evans told us herself, that if the father and the grandmother would have requested that the boy would be placed properly in kindergarten and not first grade, then it would have happened. Even now it's still not too late. My suspicions are that the grandmother here just didn't want to make any waves. She's worried she'll lose the grandson immediately if padre here gets deported."

Diane slumped back into her chair, tears in her eyes, while my son and oldest daughter leaned in to console her.

"Your Honor, I'd like to also add that what we have here with Erasmo is the poster child for what's wrong in the United States with our immigration laws. We have an illegal alien Latino who got my daughter pregnant because he thought then she'd marry him and he'd be free to stay. Yet all these years later, he still hasn't followed the steps to become legal in this country. He doesn't need a taxpayer-funded interpreter. Like the grandmother, he's playing dumb in order to appeal for your sympathy vote. He owes my daughter more than twenty thousand in back child support, which a judge in Eugene awarded her after he abandoned her and the grandson four years ago. He works under the table, pays no taxes, all while spitting in the face of America by not following our rules. He was deported once back in 2007, only to sneak back across the border in 2008. Immigration and law enforcement have repeatedly told us that he'll have to break another law in order to be deported a second time."

"This is juvenile court," interjected Judge Heron. "Mr. Freeman, it's not in my jurisdiction to determine citizenship status."

"Okay, Your Honor. Right now, DHS believes the child is better off under the father's care, at least until the mother completes her treatment program. Could you tell me something then…What's Plan B? When Erasmo gets deported again, and it's only a matter of time, what will happen?"

"Mr. Freeman, DHS will immediately reevaluate the situation and then make a determination. When two parents are involved and the one who's caring for the child has been removed from the situation, our goal is to make every effort to place the child with the second parent."

"Thank you, Your Honor. I believe the immortal words of rock 'n roll artist Sting when he says, '*The kid should be with his mother. Everybody knows that.*'"

"Thank you, Mr. Freeman. Is that all that you have?"

"One more thing. Could you explain why Judge Thomas' decisions regarding divorce don't seem to be valid in this county any longer?"

"I'm not sure what you're getting at, Mr. Freeman?"

"Judge Thomas signed off on their divorce at the end of September and due to people in this room complaining and whining to Judge Sorro, she rescinded Judge Thomas' original order."

"Mr. Freeman, this is juvenile court. I don't do divorce cases. That matter will need to be taken up with Judge Sorro and divorce court."

"Very well, Your Honor."

"Anything else, Mr. Freeman?"

"Not at this time, Your Honor."

"Anybody else?" asked Judge Heron.

Tyler stood up.

"I'm Tyler James Freeman. I'm Trystan's uncle. On behalf of Trystan and our family, I'd like to thank and commend everyone from the Ashland Police Department and Jackson County DHS. Your tireless efforts and countless work hours are appreciated. Keep doing what you're doing."

"Thank you, Mr. Freeman."

As Tyler sat down, Libby stood up.

"I'm Liberty Nicole Freeman. I go by Libby."

"Okay, Libby."

"I'm Trystan's aunt. I just want to agree with everything my brother just said."

"Is there anything else in your *own* words, Ms. Freeman?"

"I can't really think of anything in my own words right now, Your Honor. Oh, wait a minute. I just thought of something else. Like my mom always says, when it comes to his schooling, Trystan doesn't test well."

"Thank you, Ms. Freeman. Anybody else?" asked Judge Heron.

Faith stood.

"I'm Trystan's mom, Faith Freeman, Your Honor. I'd like to thank everybody including my brother, sister, parents, grandparents, Erasmo and everybody else for being here and caring so much about my son. I don't understand why life has to be so difficult all the time and I wish we could just all sit down, talk and stop fighting so much. People from broken families don't have to keep tearing each other apart."

"I'd have to agree with you, Ms. Freeman. By the way, the name, *Trystan*, seems unique. wasn't *Tristan* a knight at King Arthur's Round Table?"

"Yes, Your Honor, and it was the name of Brad Pitt's character in *Legends of the Fall. Trystan* means 'tumultuous' and an 'outcry.'"

"That seems fitting in this case."

"Your Honor, I wanted to add one more thing. There are many divorced parents who somehow get along all the time. Erasmo and I are trying to do the best we can all the time."

"I'd have to agree, while I also think it's safe to say that the role models you had as parents were not very good ones."

Sarcastic laughter echoed throughout the courtroom, even though I struggled to find the humor.

Faith continued, "Your Honor, I'm planning to move back down to Medford after Thanksgiving, so could we work out exactly what my visitation times will be for the holidays and beyond, until something changes?"

"I believe we're done now unless anybody has anything else to say… Mr. Flowers, I've determined that Trystan's case with the DHS will remain open and the child will remain under his father's direct supervision. I believe we're done now so could you, Erasmo, and Faith use the side conference room to work out a visitation schedule for the holidays and thereafter?"

"Let's do it," said Flowers.

After Faith and Erasmo exited with Flowers, I decided to take a few breaths while letting people filter out of the courtroom. I glanced over my shoulder and noticed that Diane and Libby had already departed, while Tyler was just starting to head to the door. Since he had been giving me the "silent treatment" for a number of weeks now, I decided it was time for me to get in my son's ear for a moment. I began walking out behind him. By the time we'd left the courtroom, we were side-by-side in the lobby.

"Son, how long did you say your mother told you she's been sober?"

"Dad, shut the fuck up."

"Hey, your grandmother's here, somewhere. You don't need to talk like that."

"Shut the fuck up."

"How long has she been sober, and why do you and Libby keep enabling her?"

"Dad, I said, SHUT THE FUCK UP!"

"Ty, let's go outside and talk about this."

Ty appeared to really be boiling. He came at me, and I went at him. We stopped and got right up in each other's grilles, like two prizefighters staring each other down.

"Dad, I'm going to kick your ass right here and now."

At this point my dad, Ty's grandpa, started wedging his way in between us. By then all the other Freemans except Faith had gathered around. Dad started pushing on me. Since I was wearing a suit, tie and slick dress shoes, I couldn't seem to keep my footing as I slipped toward the front door.

"GET THE HELL OUT OF HERE!" Dad shouted.

"Dad, I'm not going to fight your grandson."

"GET THE HELL OUT OF HERE!"

"Dad, I just want to ask Tyler one more question." I laughed. "I don't want to have to kick *your* ass, first!"

"Goddammit! I said get out of here!"

Dad and I walked down the street. I had ridden with him to court in his pickup truck.

When he opened the door, I reached in and grabbed my raincoat and keys.

"Dad, I need a break from you and you need to let your blood pressure drop. I'll see you later."

I then walked back to see if Faith was ready to go. As I approached the front of the court house, my son reappeared with Diane and Libby.

"Son, I have one more question."

"Keep walking, Ty," said Libby. "He's not worth it."

Tyler stopped and took off his coat, handed it to Diane and put up his hands in a fighter's position. I saw that Mr. Moralez, the security guard, had followed them out.

"There's going to be a fight," Moralez said into his shoulder mic. "I'm going to head back inside the building to contact an officer."

"Wait just a minute!" I said. "Mr. Moralez, I want you to witness this. There isn't going to be a fight."

I approached Tyler. "Son, what are you going to do? Do you *really* want to hit your dad? Go ahead, that's exactly what your mother wants."

"That's bullshit, Dad."

"Son, LISTEN THIS TIME! Did she tell you about her DUI? Do you know about the DUI?"

Tyler instantly gave me a confused look. He dropped his fist, turned to his mother and said, "Mom? Is that true? You told me you've been sober for five years."

Diane's legs buckled a bit and her eyes looked like she was about to faint.

"Your dad's making that up. There's not a DUI on my record."

"Son, I hate to tell you this but your mom's on a DUI diversion program, but that doesn't translate into making her sober on the night she got the DUI, no matter how anybody wants to spin it!"

"No shit, Dad, I'm not in denial!"

"MR. MORALEZ!" shouted Di. "ARE YOU GOING TO GET THE POLICE HERE OR DO I HAVE TO CALL 9-1-1?"

I stared straight into my son's eyes, winked, then turned and hit the sidewalk. I walked around the block, back to the motel room, packed my stuff, drove the car back to the court building, picked Faith up and then took her back to Eugene.

The following Monday afternoon, I got a phone call from Dad.

"Hello, Dad."

"Listen Billy, I'd like to apologize about what happened on Thursday. I just didn't want you to end up in jail for fighting with your son."

"Dad, I will never hit Tyler, especially with the first punch. He knows that and one of the reasons he won't throw the first punch, on anybody, is because I've taught him the seriousness of Measure 11 crimes, particularly assault. The kid has too much to lose."

"I know, and that is something he's taken to heart."

"Dad, I accept your apology. It's water under the bridge."

"Okay, good, Son. Now, there's something you need to do tomorrow."

"What's that, Dad?"

"I did some checking. You need to call the Jackson County Circuit Court Tuesday morning at nine. Just give the receptionist your name and ask her if there's anything you need to be aware of."

"Dad? What's going on?"

"Just do what I say and don't call in late."

I followed my dad's advice. The receptionist put me through to a Judge Black. Jesus, I thought. Is this court stuff ever going to end?

"Mr. Freeman, this is Judge Black."

"Good morning, Your Honor."

"I now have you on speaker phone. A Ms. Diane Christine Downer, your ex-wife, is joining us in the courtroom today. Do you know why we're here?"

"I could speculate, Your Honor, but I don't want to do that."

"You are being issued a temporary restraining order."

"Your Honor, are you aware that she's already tried to pull this before? Last year in Portland and the judge up there immediately dismissed it because she had no basis for filing it?"

"I'm not aware of that."

"Well, could we just ask if Ms. Downer wants to drop this?"

"This is for a show-cause hearing. You get a chance to accept or deny the charges. If you deny, then we'll set a date for a formal hearing. She'll be able to drop things prior to the formal hearing if she decides."

"Okay, Your Honor."

"I have an Oregon Uniform Stalking Complaint before me. It was written up by Ashland Police Officer Vaughn Seward. The petitioner is Diane Christine Downer and the respondent is William Blake Freeman. The petitioner alleges that the respondent threatened to run her over with his car, sent e-mail and text message threats. The petitioner alleges that respondent came to her home after being told numerous times she did not want contact with him. Petitioner alleges that respondent went through her trash and waited for her to come home and threatened to run her over with his car. Respondent delivered message through son that petitioner recommended she not show up for a court hearing and texted her: 'Your days are numbered.' Ms. Downer, are these statements accurate and did you sign this complaint?"

"Yes and yes."

"Mr. Freeman, do you accept or deny the charges."

"Deny, Your Honor."

"Then we need to set a hearing date. Can you appear in the morning on December 24, Mr. Freeman?"

"Christmas Eve, Your Honor?"

"Justice doesn't take time off, Mr. Freeman, but if you really want to we could do it in January."

"No, Your Honor, I'd rather get this over with so we could put 2010 behind us and look forward to the new year. I'll be there on Christmas Eve."

"Does that date work for you, Ms. Downer?"

"Uhhh, sure Your Honor. My family will be with me for Christmas in Ashland this year, so that date will be just fine."

CHAPTER 6:

"Permanent" Stalking Order

As I continued my sabbatical from financial advising in the Portland area to focus on my writing career and triathlon training, I decided to return to the High Desert Cascades of Central Oregon. I relocated to Bend, my homeland, where I was raised by two elementary school teachers. Bend was recently chosen as one of *Triathlete Magazine's* top ten "Best Places to Train." I perceived returning after more than twenty years away as an exhilarating and refreshing opportunity.

I was not pleased cutting into my training time while driving from Bend to Medford for a Christmas Eve date in court. The road conditions were hazardous, traffic was heavy, and the pass near Crater Lake National Park had been dumped on with a fresh foot of snow. What normally takes about three hours to drive in the spring and summer took nearly double that amount of time. Megan Love, my dear friend, bedroom aerobics instructor, and triathlon training partner, joined me on the drive, providing insight, intelligence and her calming reflective spirit which had been crucial in helping me keep sane throughout this entire ordeal.

The Honorable Judge Donald Ronski presided over the festivities at the Jackson County Circuit Court in Medford. From the computer screen in the court house lobby, Judge Ronski's docket appeared extra full on this day. I still didn't know why court was scheduled on a Friday before Christmas but the flyers next to the elevator indicated that court would not be in session on Monday, instead. Southern Oregon always seemed a bit backwards to me when I lived there, so I guess this wasn't anything different.

I noticed a familiar-looking attorney though his name initially escaped me. It didn't take long for my memory to be refreshed as he immediately handed me some documents after Megan and I sat down on the left side of the courtroom.

"Mr. Freeman?"

"Yes."

"I'm Franklin For...

"Foreskin!" I interrupted...

"Actually, it's *Fortran*...like the computer language."

"That's right. Sorry, Fortran. Now I remember you. You represented Diane in the custody case with Tyler."

"Yes, Mr. Freeman, and I also remember you from playing basketball at the gym."

"That's right."

"So, I'm representing Ms. Downer again, today."

"All right. Good luck."

I handed the stack of documents to Megan. As Diane, Tyler and Libby entered the courtroom and took a position on the opposite side of the courtroom, Megan started scanning the stack.

A few minutes later, Meg leaned over next to me and whispered, "There are at least fifty pages of phone records and a printout from your Facebook page and some e-mail messages between you and Faith. How did Diane get e-mails from between you and Faith?"

"Good question."

Judge Ronski entered the courtroom. Everyone stood. I noticed Faith enter the court room and take a seat in the center between us and the other side. I immediately felt my phone vibrate. It was a text message from Faith.

Dad,
If you call me up to talk today, you know I'm going to tell the truth. I just want to look neutral by sitting by myself so they won't think you're influencing what I say.

Works for me, I thought. I also thought that I now had three choices to make. First, I could go through with this hearing without an attorney like I did a year ago in Portland. I could call a time-out and ask for a rescheduling since the evidence was given to me in a non-timely fashion. I could take on Mr. Fortran with the same tenacity I took him to the hole, schooling him in hoops at the gym, and while pulling from the words and the spirit of Abraham Lincoln when he said, "The probability that we may fail in the struggle ought not to deter us from the support of the cause we believe to be just." I asked myself, what's the worst that could happen? I might lose today, but the way our justice system is designed there would always be room for...

The Appeal of Stalking.

I was a bit surprised that our case was called first.

Fortran called Officer Vaughn Seward as a witness and then Diane. I objected a number of times and asked Officer Seward why he hadn't called me back after he received my forwarded e-mails from Diane. He sloughed off my questions by saying that Diane's e-mail was spam and he's gotten that from her before.

Next up was Diane. She appeared nervous. Judge Ronski asked her to state her full name for the record.

"I'm Diane Downer."

"Could you move into the mic a little closer and enunciate," said Ronski. "And did you say your name is Diane Downs?"

"Enunciate?"

"Speak more clearly, please."

Diane moved closer to the mic.

"No, Your Honor. I am *not* Diane Downs. It's *Downer*. My last name is Downer. My full name is Diane Christine Downer."

"Okay, Ms. Downer. Thank you."

Diane performed the same routine she'd performed in Portland thirteen months earlier, complete with tears and no eye contact whatsoever. She said that she was afraid. When Fortran asked her why she was "afraid of Mr. Freeman," she replied, "I'm afraid that Billy will end my life."

This string of lies kept going. I lost count at twenty. My strategy was to work through the lies and argue that I had not violated what was being alleged.

As I pleaded my side of the case, my goal was to stick to the issues of the alleged stalking complaint. "In response, please let me state for the record: I did not go through her garbage. I did not take pictures of her alcohol consumption. I did not try to run her over with my car. I did not send her threatening e-mails, texts, or phone messages."

"Mr. Freeman, we are here to prove one thing and one thing only," said Judge Ronski.

"And that's whether or not you had unwanted contact which alarmed or coerced the petitioner."

"Your Honor, we went through this in Portland last year. Judge Maureen McKnight made it very clear that 'unwanted' does not mean 'unnecessary,' 'prohibited,' or that I wasn't allowed to voice my opinion of and to Ms. Downer."

"I've already acknowledged that the hearing in Portland in November of 2009 was dismissed. We're not here to discuss any more of what happened in Portland, Mr. Freeman. Now, I want to let you get your case in but I've got a lot of other cases to get to today so we need to expedite this to discover whether or not you are guilty of unwanted contact."

"Okay, Your Honor, I did not go through Ms. Downer's garbage. I did not try to run her over with my car. I did not send her threatening texts, e-mails or phone messages. I am NOT guilty of bogus stalking charges. I AM guilty of two things. The first is defending my daughter by helping her with her God-given American citizen's right of getting a divorce finalized, to rid herself of a marriage gone awry to an illegal alien non-American citizen.

"And the second thing, Mr. Freeman?"

"I'm guilty of loving my grandson. Loving my grandson enough to stick up for him and speak out in his defense in order that ill-advised, unintelligent people in his life won't do major damage to his impressionable psyche by not doing what's in his best interests regarding his educational grade-level placement."

"It sounds to me like neither of you want contact, so what's the big deal if I impose a permanent stalking protective order against you?"

"What's the *Big Deal,* Your Honor? I am proud of my clean record with no criminal history. Ms. Downer should not be allowed to soil me any longer! If anybody should have a stalking protective order against another, it's me against her! Could I allege that she stalked me thirty years ago in high school? Could I allege that she stalked me and trapped me into marrying her when I was a teenager? Could I allege that she stalked me toward financial ruin, without any remorse whatsoever? I could, but I'm not going to go there. I simply wish to be allowed to escape and go free. I want my American freedom of expression and if her actions negatively impact my family and friends—those people close to me—I should be allowed to voice my First Amendment rights! If I'm guilty of anything, it's the following...Again, I'm guilty of loving my grandson *and* my kids...

"I did not have contact with this woman for almost six months and when I finally did, it was simply because I thought she should know that *our* daughter was in the hospital. Six weeks later, I contacted Ms. Downer simply because I love my grandson and I'm not angry, but I am passionate about the boy's placement in school and can we just acknowledge that she arranged for the kid to skip kindergarten? Your Honor, I am not guilty of stalking Diane Downer!"

The judge then let Faith take the stand to retell the story of what happened at her mother's apartment and that I had not gone through her mother's trash, tried to run her over, or taken the open container photos because Faith had taken them. Later, I attempted to call Tyler to the stand to revisit what happened weeks earlier at the Juvenile Court regarding his mother's DUI. Judge Ronski denied my request.

"Mr. Freeman, the court finds that without legitimate purpose, you intentionally, knowingly, or recklessly engaged in repeated and unwanted contact with Ms. Diane Christine Downer and thereby alarmed or coerced Ms. Downer. The court finds that it is objectively reasonable for a person in Ms. Diane Christine Downer's situation to have been alarmed or coerced by your contact and that the repeated and unwanted contact caused Ms. Downer reasonable apprehension regarding her personal safety.

"It is hereby ordered that you are prohibited from intentionally, knowingly or recklessly having contact with Diane Christine Downer and this order is of unlimited duration. Do you understand this ruling, Mr. Freeman?"

"I understand, but I don't agree with it, Your Honor."

"We'll take a ten-minute recess," said Judge Ronski as he slammed his gavel and dashed out of the courtroom.

As I was gathering my notes, Fortran approached.

"Franklin, what did the judge mean by 'unlimited duration'? Can she renege on this and have it rescinded?"

Fortran laughed as a puzzled look appeared on his face. "It's going to be a while."

"So, a year, three years?"

"I'd give it at least that long."

"All right."

"Are you still playing basketball, Billy?"

"I'm actually doing triathlons."

"Triathlons, wow. Where and when's your next one?"

"Ironman Australia, Port Macquarie in May."

"Do you fly into Sydney or Brisbane?"

"Either one. The triathlon is on the coast, right in the middle. I did Brisbane in 2008 so I think I'm going via Sydney this time."

"Make sure you see Coogee Bay. I was at Dolphins Point in 2003 just after the memorial was dedicated to the victims of the Bali terrorist bombings."

"Wow, Dolphins Point? I'm supposed to go running there. A friend of mine once invited me."

"Don't tell me she's blonde, long legs and blue eyes."

"Don't forget the accent."

"No way, mate!"

"Hey, are you still hitting the gym?"

"Bro, what's it look like, I'm in the best shape I've ever been. I can probably take you one-on-one right now!"

"Just like you did with Judge Ronski?"

We both laughed.

"I'll see you at OZ Fitness later today, and we'll go double or nothing for beers," I added.

"I'll be there, just not sure I'd show up if I were you. I'll be there at one o'clock for lunchtime basketball action. Hey, either way, for not having gone to law school, you gave a valiant performance today."

"No shit, Fortran?"

"Would I bullshit you?"

"You fuckin' attorneys are all alike," I laughed. "Especially the ones who went to law school at Oregon State."

"Billy, for the record, I went to Oregon. Oregon State doesn't have a law school."

"Damn, could have sworn, Fortran. You play basketball like you went to Oregon State."

"I'll see you on the court."

"Later, Fortran."

I noticed Officer Seward was waiting at the door. I thought that was odd because after his testimony, Judge Ronski dismissed him and said he could return to Ashland for work. I noticed that my ex-wife was out in the lobby and since I had just been ordered with a permanent stalking protective order I decided to stay in the courtroom a bit longer.

A few minutes later the bailiff said we had to go to get the final paperwork at the window downstairs. I told him that I didn't want to violate anything by going out there by the ex-wife, and that's why I was waiting.

Eventually, he said we had to go, now. So I decided to walk out anyway.

Immediately, Officer Seward approached and said, "Billy, you're under arrest for stalking."

What the fuck?

"Vaughn, I want to call an attorney."

As I reached into my pocket to pull out my phone, another officer approached:

"Keep your hands out of your pockets."

I complied as Vaughn clamped the cuffs on me.

I thought it odd that I was being arrested in the first place, and also that Officer Vaughn Seward did not read me my rights.

We approached the elevator as my ex-wife's co-workers took pictures and used their cell phones to capture the proceedings. Faith started speaking to Vaughn. I'll admit I felt a little numb and dizzy at the moment because this was the only time I had ever been arrested in my life.

On the first floor at the check-out window, we awaited the paperwork from the hearing. Officer Seward asked me if I had any sharp objects or weapons on me. I replied, "Now, wouldn't that be a little weird if I had a weapon on me since I had to go through security this morning to get into the court-room?"

"Yeah, but I guess I always ask that question."

After we received the paperwork, Officer Seward walked me over to the metal detector and removed the items from my pockets: my phone, my money/credit card clip, a pair of sun-glasses and a pen.

Megan, my girl, was a great face to see through all of this adversity.

"Vaughn, could Megan here be allowed to take my money and credit card clip?"

"Sure."

"Meg, please call Kivel and Howard's office. Someone there can tell you the easiest way to bail me out. The firm's business card is in my money clip."

"Will do, baby," Meg said. "You'll be out of here in no time."

Officer Seward escorted me outside and toward the fence outside the Jackson County Jail.

"Vaughn, I still don't know why you are arresting me."

"I believe you are stalking your ex-wife. Besides, you broke the stalking order."

"I was never served a stalking citation."

"You broke the order the day that my partner served you."

"Vaughn, where were you? He never served me a stalking citation."

"You were served."

"Vaughn, I know how it is to get served. I *was* served in Portland at my office last year. The cop there followed procedures and the process. The appropriate procedures were not followed in this case."

"I'm just going by what was written in my partner's police report."

"Well, his police report isn't accurate. Where were YOU, Vaughn?"

"We have limited resources. We only had three officers on duty and I had to appear before a grand jury."

"When the other officer approached me, he asked me if I was Billy Freeman. I nodded my head and asked him if he was 'Officer Seward?' He replied 'No,' but he added that he had been asked to come in your place. I immediately told him that I would not be talking to him until I first spoke with my attorney. I turned and walked away. I headed toward the door and as he started mumbling, I told him that I could not hear or understand a word he was saying and I proceeded to go outside, turned right. After I was about half of a block away, I realized that he had chosen not to follow me."

A few seconds of silence passed, and then I continued, "Where were you, Vaughn? You told you me on the phone you work three, twelve-hour shifts on Mondays through Wednesdays. Again, that was a Thursday."

"I also work on every-other Thursday. It's just easier for me not to tell people that. When I'd attempt to tell people straight up, they'd call on Thursdays and expect return calls and their calls would usually happen on the Thursdays that I wasn't working. The callers would get upset, so it's just better for me to say that I just work on Monday through Wednesdays."

"So why are you working today? It's Friday."

Officer Seward didn't respond to this question. Instead, he changed the subject...

"I think what your daughter was saying outside of the elevator was out of line and incredibly disrespectful."

"Why is that?" I said.

"She was asking me how I knew her mother and was implying that her mother and I had some sort of relationship. Did you hear her?"

"Vaughn, have I been disrespectful through this whole process? Didn't I return your calls?"

"Not always timely, but yes you did."

"Wasn't I respectful in the courtroom today in the way I questioned you?"

"Yes, you were."

"So was I respectful through this whole process to you?"

"Yes you were, but your daughter wasn't. She was implying that I had a relationship with your ex-wife. With her mother."

"Listen, Vaughn. Her mother has some severe issues. You probably don't know this but her mother slept with one of my teenage students when I was a high school English teacher. She didn't tell anybody for seven years. So if my daughter asked you or implied anything regarding your relationship— I didn't hear exactly what she said—my daughter was not being far-fetched... If my daughter was questioning your relationship with her mom, I see nothing wrong with that. And I don't even know why you're making such a big issue out of it. Perhaps my daughter is onto something?"

Officer Seward stayed silent.

I immediately began pondering several questions.

Why was a City of Ashland police officer arresting me when I had not been officially, legally, and lawfully served an *Oregon Uniform Stalking Citation*?

Why was a City of Ashland police officer arresting me in the City of Medford?

Why was a City of Ashland police officer arresting me without an arrest warrant?

How did Officer Vaughn Seward know that Faith was my daughter, especially after Officer Seward left the courtroom immediately following his testimony, which was the first testimony that was heard?

The following is Faith's recollection of her experience with Officer Vaughn Seward...

I was visiting my son, Trystan, at my mother's home on December 10, when I asked her:

"Are you still dating that guy you told me you were seeing earlier in the year?"

"Who do you think?"

"Mom. Didn't you say his name was Bruce?"

"Why are you asking?" she replied. "Is this about Officer Seward?"

"What do you mean? Is Bruce, Officer Seward?"

"No, I'm just wondering why you're asking that. I hesitate with court coming up. You may be trying to get information for your dad."

"No, I said you could trust me, after welcoming me into your home. I told you I'm not here to hurt you. I was just curious and trying to make conversation."

I began pondering why my mom would bring up Officer Seward completely out of the blue, when I asked a simple question. It made me curious as to whether or not my mom was a friend of Officer Seward. Maybe Officer Seward is friends with Bruce? Maybe my mom brought up Officer Seward because I had asked about her relationship status? Could my mother be having a relationship with Officer Seward?

Many questions went through my mind, but I immediately brushed them off until December 24, when Officer Seward took the stand.

My dad brought up e-mails he had received from my mom that he later forwarded to Officer Seward, questioning why she might have sent him e-mails during the temporary restraining order time period.

When pressed about my mom's e-mail contact, and why Officer Seward hadn't called him (my dad) back, Officer Seward replied, "It was spam. I get the same e-mails from her all the time."

He is friends with my mom! Why else would he be getting e-mail from her and why else would he be on her e-mail group list?

I immediately texted Dad's girlfriend, Megan.

"That cop must know Mom, personally."

After court, Officer Seward put my dad in handcuffs and the events that I witnessed immediately afterward were perplexing…

Officer Vaughn Seward's attitude and demeanor was not that of a cop who was "just doing his job." It was personal.

Although I'm not proud of myself, I've been arrested a number of times and I'd never seen anything like this before.

Officer Seward was enjoying himself. My instincts tell me that he had been preparing for this moment. It was as if he had been coached by my mom.

I also recall my mom asking me how she could drop this nonsense. I told her that she only needed to send a letter to the judge. I even showed her an example. She made a phone call after the conversation at her house when the topic of Officer Seward had been brought up. I overheard that phone call and she was talking to someone about dropping the temporary restraining order. The person on the other end seemed to be laying out all of the possible outcomes of the hearing.

So as Officer Seward was walking out with my dad, I blurted out to him, "This is a joke. You know my mom, don't you?"

"What are you talking about?" he replied.

"Or maybe you know her boyfriend. Maybe you are her boyfriend?"

I couldn't put my finger on what I was trying to say, but I felt in my heart that some kind of set-up had taken place, right before my eyes. Something was sketchy.

"Who's your mom's boyfriend?" he asked.

"It doesn't matter," I said. "But something's not right here. Something is going on."

As I started to move away from Officer Seward and my dad, Officer Seward started raising his voice.

"Tell me who your mom's boyfriend is and I can tell you if I know him."

I stayed silent and continued to walk away as he shouted even louder, "WHO IS YOUR MOM'S BOYFRIEND?"

I left and began wondering why he was so concerned about who my mom's boyfriend is, and why he was so uncomfortable when I implied that he knew my mom outside of the courtroom...

A cherry red Honda Del Sol drove by us with the windows down as Officer Seward finished escorting me across the parking lot toward the Jackson County Jail. I smirked as I recognized a familiar song coming from its stereo...

It was a song sung by Scott Stapp...Classic Creed...

Court is in session
A verdict is in
No appeal on the docket today
Just my own sin...

Officer Seward then turned me over to two Jackson County Sheriff's deputies. He broke his silence for one final comment. "Merry Christmas, Billy. I hope you get to spend time with your family."

I looked him in the eyes, stared his ass down, nodded, and then winked.

The deputies led me down a cold hall to receive my jail clothes. I was issued green scrubs, a pair of bright orange Crocs, and pink cotton underwear. Funny, this must be some sort of derogatory, yet humbling psychological tactic, I thought. However, it had no effect on me because I've never had a problem wearing pink. I wore a bright pink sweater during a high school basketball game I was coaching on Valentine's Day in 1990 in Salem. After an incredible victory, I realized that it was still relatively early and I looked forward to spending time that evening with my wife. I realized there was a problem when I got home around ten p.m., and neither she, nor the kids—who should have been in their beds sleeping—were home. There was a message from her on the answering machine. Diane's car had broken down on I-5 so I grabbed my truck and a chain, drove forty-five minutes back to Salem, and then towed her car. Thus, our "romantic" Valentine's Day celebration was to no avail.

I also wore long pink shorts and a pink baseball cap when I was directing and participating in the Southern Oregon Jam three-on-three basketball tournament in the nineties in Ashland. I was even interviewed and recorded by numerous Medford television stations while wearing pink.

I also remember meeting Noel, a hair stylist posing as a psychic, online. She had agreed to meet me for dinner on a weekend. Over the phone prior to dinner, she correctly told me that I had worn a blue shirt on Thursday and then a green shirt on Friday. I told her not to tell me what color I was wearing on Saturday night until I called her five minutes prior to meeting her. I had brought a red Hawaiian shirt and a pink-colored shirt with contrasting lined patterns that my son Tyler had given me for Father's Day. Turns out it was originally

Tyler's shirt. He had worn it once but I guess some friends of his accused him of being (in his words) a "homo" so he didn't want to wear it any more.

After I finished parking my truck, I decided to go all out with the pink shirt. Then I called her on my cell phone.

"Noel, are you at the martini bar, yet?"

"Yes. I just got here."

"Are you ready to tell me the color of my shirt?"

"Yes, but I must say that today was a struggle. All that kept coming back to me throughout the last few hours was red. But something is telling me now that red just isn't the one. I'm feeling a softer tone of red. Pink is a color which many guys don't feel comfortable in. Something to do with sexuality. It's like if you wear pink and you are a guy then you aren't masculine."

By that time I started walking down the sidewalk to the bar. We continued our conversation.

"Noel, my son says that men who wear pink are 'faggots.' What do you think?"

"On the contrary. I know why he might say that, because he's young and inexperienced. Did Dire Straits wear pink when they sang 'that little *faggot* with the earring and the make-up' in *Money for Nothing and Chicks for Free*? Nahhh. But I think that men who are secure in their masculinity wear pink, purple, even the full colors of the rising sun."

"I'd have to agree."

Noel laughed.

"So are you wearing pink?"

I laughed as I entered the bar. Across the crowded room, we recognized each other immediately.

So my reaction was a little ironic when the sheriff's deputy gave me a pink T-shirt for my first-ever mug shot: Tyler's going to love this one, I thought.

After the mug shot, it was onto fingerprinting.

Big fucking deal, I thought. I have been fingerprinted by at least three school districts for teaching and coaching. I'd also been fingerprinted for my job as a financial advisor for A.G. Edwards, Wachovia, and Wells Fargo Advisors.

After fingerprinting, I was given bedding and then placed into a detainment cell.

As I entered, one grimy, greasy Charles Manson look-alike crawled under his blankets atop a bench on the opposite end of the room from me, while a youthful inmate sat staring at the ceiling from the bench on the other side.

I sat across from the young inmate. He looked about 6'3", 190 pounds. He appeared to be in his early-to-mid twenties. He had a well-groomed beard, clean-cut hair and a quiet disposition. The only disturbing part of him was the ear-to-ear scar which ran across his neck. He looked over at me.

"So what did you do?" he asked.

"I'm still trying to figure it out, myself. I just finished up with a civil case for a permanent restraining order. I walked out of the courtroom and an Ashland cop slapped cuffs on me and said I was being arrested for stalking."

"Ashland cop," he laughed. "Who were you stalking?"

"Ex-wife…errr…I wasn't stalking her. This is my first time, EVER, in jail."

"Damn, if they nail you with a stalking felony charge, you're toast. You can't own a weapon, you can't vote or leave the state without permission, and if you have a passport, you can kiss that goodbye for life!"

I broke a sweat after his last comments. No leaving the state? Shit, I'm supposed to go to the BCS championship in Phoenix. Downer's even trying to keep me from seeing my Ducks go for the crystal trophy. No passport? No Australian Ironman Triathlon. No running at Coogee Bay? Jesus!

"Like I said, I wasn't stalking her."

"That's what we all say. Are you from Ashland?"

"Not anymore," I replied. "I lived there with my family in the nineties. Are you from Ashland?"

"Yeah."

"Are you working there?"

"Yeah. I cook breakfast at Munchies."

"Munchies? Is it still in the Plaza?"

"Yeah."

"I love Munchies. Especially their giant German chocolate cakes. What's your name?"

"Aaron."

"Hi Aaron, I'm Billy."

I reached out my hand to him and we exchanged a quick handshake.

"Did you go to Ashland High?"

"Yeah."

"What year did you graduate?"

"I would have in 2006, but I wrote a paper for my senior project and I guess the administration didn't look too kindly on the topic."

"What?"

"Yeah, I got expelled in my last semester."

"What was your essay about?"

"It was titled, *Why Teachers Should be Allowed to Carry Concealed Weapons in Schools.*"

"Wasn't there a teacher from Medford who was fighting that same fight?"

"Yeah, she's actually my mom's friend, Shirley. Her ex-husband wouldn't stop stalking her so she started bringing her semi-automatic 9mm Glock to North Medford High. I actually got the idea for the paper from Mrs. Katz. She teaches English."

"No shit? Is Mrs. Katz, Shirley?"

"Yeah, she and my mom are teaching buddies."

"Did Mrs. Katz have a concealed weapons permit?"

"Yep."

"So, let me get this straight, Aaron. You got kicked out of school for writing a paper?"

"Yeah, I was expressing my opinion."

"That doesn't seem quite right, especially in Ashland. People seemed to have open minds there; at least they did when I lived there. Is that all of your story?"

"Well, I had gotten busted earlier for selling pot and that affected my reputation. People weren't as forgiving after that."

"So what did you do?"

"I got my G.E.D. and then went to University of Cal at San Diego to study bio-engineering."

"So how old are you, Aaron? You must be about twenty-two?"

"Twenty-three, actually."

"You're the same age as my son. Wait, do you know my son, Tyler?"

"Tyler Freeman or Fieguth?"

"Freeman."

"Of course, everybody from Ashland knows Tyler, and his older sisters Libby and Faith. They were all great athletes. I'm even Facebook friends with all of them."

"What's your last name, Aaron?"

"It's Pastor."

"Aaron Pastor…Don't you have a sister named Jessica?"

"Yeah."

"And weren't you and Tyler in school together?"

"Not until sixth grade at Ashland Middle School. I went to Lincoln Elementary, Ty went to Bellview."

"That's right."

"What happened to Tyler? I remember he left high school at the start of our junior year."

"He got busted for selling pot."

"No shit? I heard he went to play basketball in Idaho."

"He did go there to play basketball, more importantly, to graduate from high school, but the catalyst was that he was pulled over while driving his mother's SUV. The cops found two pounds of pot, baggies, scales and almost two thousand in cash in the console and another thousand in his pocket. The police report even said that his mother claimed that the cash was hers, and she wanted it back."

"Isn't his mother's name Diane?"

"Yeah."

"Well, I hate to tell you this. But your son wasn't the one selling that pot."

"Huh, then who was?"

"Wake up, man. His mom, of course! So that cash probably *was* hers. She not only sold pot, but she was also selling pharmaceutical sample drugs from Ashland Family Care and Del Norte Family Practice. All the kids in town knew that if they wanted speed or anti-depressants that Diane Freeman was the local supplier. I heard she liked the attention from the high school boys. The drug-samples cupboards at the doctors' offices were like the candy store to her."

"Last spring I did ask Tyler's buddy, Alex, who was in the car when he was busted, if Ty's mother was selling pot with him."

"What'd he say?"

"He said that 'Tyler is his best friend' and he didn't feel comfortable talking about it."

"Ty probably took the hit for his mom, since the crime only ended up on his juvenile record. She would have gone to prison for years on felony charges."

"Aaron, why are you in here, now?" I asked.

"I was brought here three days ago from the hospital. They think I tried to kill myself."

He drew a finger over the top of his scar.

"So they brought you to jail?"

"No, I'm in here for probation violations."

"Probation violations?"

"Yeah, I just didn't show up to court regarding the pot charges. Everything has kind of snowballed now."

I motioned to my neck with my finger and drew a line across my neck.

"So where did this happen?"

"Oh, I was on the tennis courts at Southern Oregon University."

"No shit. Do you know who?"

"Yeah. I know, but I'll never tell. Four detectives visited my hospital room and they were all fired up. Most of them were talking attempted suicide, but they were also mentioning attempted homicide."

"Did you owe him money?"

"It wasn't a *him*. *She* is the love of my life."

"Damn."

"I know, and all I can remember is her shouting at me right before she slit my throat!"

"What was she shouting?"

"Two things. First, she said, *'STOP LOOKING AT OTHER WOMEN!'*"

"And the second?"

"She said, *'STOP STALKING ME!'*"

The conversation with Aaron was almost surreal. All I could think of was how this kid sitting across the cell from me could be my son, Tyler. If Tyler's grandparents and I hadn't gotten him out of Ashland, he was just a probation violation away from being in here and having his neck slit by some crazed girl who didn't want him looking at other girls *and* who didn't want him stalking her. My son was the lucky one. Leaving Ashland saved his life. He got away from his mother selling drugs. He got away from using drugs. He graduated from high school and got a job as a forest fire fighter the summer out of high school. He spent five months in the woods all over the western U.S., working sixteen-hour days, eating well, saving his money and most importantly, taking his life by the horns and regrouping. The skills he learned outside of Southern Oregon carried him to a year of college, and even though I would have liked for him to continue, he moved out of college and into the business world where he could sell, LEGALLY!

"Aaron, someday I'd like to read your essay. Did you save a copy of it?"

"Yeah, I have it on a disk somewhere. When I get out of here I can e-mail it to you. Are you on Facebook?"

"Yeah. I'll look forward to getting it from you."

As Aaron shifted toward taking a nap, I began to ponder. I had become dazed with this, my first visit inside a jail cell…

...What happened to my son? He was doing so well. He started selling flat-screen televisions at the Lloyd Center Mall in Portland. One of his customers who bought a TV from him had recently accepted a sales management position with a new mobile Internet company. She was so impressed with Tyler's sales skills that she told him right there in the electronics department that she wanted to hire him and he was coming with her. Six months later, Tyler was the top sales rep throughout Portland for CLEAR Mobile Internet. He even made plans to open his own store on Lombard Avenue, while also generating great income with Internet sales in other metropolitan areas in the U.S.

The last dinner my son and I had together prior to the Dancin' Bare, was on 9/9/09. His friend, Josh, joined us as did Megan and Ty's girlfriend, Holly. Tyler looked me straight in the eye and said, "Dad, I'm killing it on my website. In addition to the Portland business, I'm selling mobile Internet in Atlanta and Vegas, weeks ahead of the main company release."

"That's great, Sonshine. So the company is okay with this?"

"Yeah. At least until we go fully nationwide."

"When will that be?"

"In about two years. Dad, I ran the numbers. In the next twenty-four months, I will be making $935,000 a year, that's just off the website. It doesn't count my regular sales rep position, nor the store."

"Nine-hundred thirty-five thousand? Sounds like you found a job you could make drug money and you're actually doing things legally?"

"Exactly, Dad."

"How's Libby working out with the phone sales and the walk-ins at the store? I know when you opened last month, you were a little concerned if she could handle the pressure."

"She's tearing things up and she keeps up for the most part but she's getting slammed with calls from eight to eight!

"Sounds like maybe you might have to hire another employee."

"I just did."

"Oh yeah, who?"

"Dad, I know you're not going to like it...but I hired Mom."

"Son, you're right. I don't like it. I don't think it's a very good idea. Letting her get involved in family business has always spelled disaster for her and everyone around her."

After almost eighteen years of marriage to his mother, I knew what her potential was to mess with a guy's businesses. I watched three of my businesses go in the tank after taking her "advice." I watched her second husband burst into tears after he got canned when she didn't want to move to another part of the state, after he had earned a promotion. Instead, twenty-five years with the same company went up in smoke. So I wasn't surprised when three weeks after my son shared his (almost) two-million dollar earnings forecast that he not only was forced to immediately shut down his website, but he was also forced to close down the store. Fortunately for him, he was allowed to keep his original sales rep job, and his mother was forced to leave Portland and return to Southern Oregon...

The sound of the cell door being unlocked brought me out of my daze.

"FREEMAN," said the guard, "It's time to go upstairs."

"Upstairs" was the bunk room. I counted about forty inmates. More than half of them were Mexicans as evidenced by the crowd gathered around the one television set which was blasting a Spanish channel.

And talk about a small world, but the only three black guys currently in jail, Sedale, DeShawn, and Danny, were Tyler's friends. Their eyes all lit up and they smiled when they saw me approach an open bunk next to them.

"GET OUTTA TOWN, HOMEY!"

"DeShawn, whazzup?" I asked. "Danny, and Sedale, how are my boyz?"

"It's Skizzle's dad!" said Danny.

"Fo Shiiiiiiit!" said Sedale.

"Damn, BillyMan!" said DeShawn. "Why is yo white ass in here?"

"Skizzle's mother said I was stalking her."

"Momma Diane did that?" asked Sedale.

"Bitch sounds like she needs to be slapped!" said Danny.

"Why are you guys in here?"

"FO SLAPPIN' BITCHES!" yelled DeShawn.

We all started howling!

"Remember that time a few years ago in Eugene when we were at Skizzle's?" asked Danny.

"You mean for March Madness?" I asked.

"Yeah," he continued. "Homies, you should have seen Skizzle's. We were all drinking forties and Skizzlie's dad here stops by and Alex, Josh, Morgan, Beau, Justin, Nick and even Faith were all there. Anyway, you should have seen it! In just a few minutes Billy here sets up three fuckin' laptops to go along with Skizzle's big flat screen and get this, motherfuckers...I'm not shitting you motherfuckers, we watched ALL sixteen motherfuckin' games on Thursday, and all sixteen motherfuckin' games on Friday."

"No shit?" asked Sedale. "Sixteen motherfuckin' games?"

"Both days," said Danny. "No Shit."

"Where were you, DeShawn?" asked Sedale.

"I was still in the state pen," said DeShawn. "Oh Billy-Man, I never got to thank you for writing those letters to me and sending me those books. There were a lot of days when I was really depressed and even thought about suicide, but I'd just read your letters and those books and what you did got me through. That book about the farmer kid who got his arms cut off in the machinery and he somehow ran a mile across the field with blood spurting everywhere and even though he was about to bleed to death he kept going and he survived."

"DeShawn, that's one of my favorites, as well."

"What was that called again, Billy?"

"*A Measure of Endurance*, by Steven Sharp."

"That's it! So thank you, Billy, my dad was never there for me and I appreciate what you did."

"DeShawn, we all slip up in life. I was just being there for you, like I try to be for all of my kids and their friends."

"Skizzle's lucky to have you for his dad," added DeShawn.

"Yeah, no shit, mofo," added Danny.

"Thanks."

"Hey Billy? Do you still ball?" asked DeShawn.

"I do. I'm supposed to be going at it against Diane's attorney Franklin Fortran over at OZ Fitness today but I don't think I'll be out of here before one. DeShawn, why do you ask?"

"We made the finals of the annual Jackson County Jail Holiday Three-on-Three basketball tournament. Danny sprained his ankle yesterday, so we need a replacement. Are you still shooting 3's like Skizzle?"

"DeShawn, you know...they can take away your freedom, but they can't take away your jump shot!"

"Great, 'cause we're playing the guards."

"It's just like that movie, *The Longest Yard*, only driveway-style basketball," said Sedale.

"What do we wear for shoes? We don't have to play in these Crocs?"

"Oh, they'll check shoes out to us down at the court," said Deshawn.

"Who are the guards we're playing?"

"Oh, nigga Sedale don't fuckin' know what he's talkin' about. They're not really guards, they're ringers that the county brings in," said Danny...three local homies...I think their names are Manny Crump, Kirk Daley and James Van Hook."

"No shit. Those guys used to play in the three-on-three we had in Ashland and I think they played city league for Gepetto's Restaurant as well! They can ball!"

"We can take them," said Sedale. "But we'd better be bringing our 'A' game."

"I don't know about you guys, I'll play, but I won't be doing any bitch-slapping on the court. I don't need to get called for a flagrant assault charge out there. I'm hoping to be bailed out of here before tonight so I can get home for Christmas."

CHAPTER 7:

The Stalking Attorney

DeShawn, Sedale and I found ourselves in a three-on-three battle at the Jackson County Jail basketball court against Manny, James and the always goofy 6'8" beanpole, Kirk. Although Manny had lost a step since I last played against him in the Southern Oregon Jam in 2002, he still could shoot the three.

The winning team would be rewarded with what Danny said was a "legit Christmas dinner" from the All-You-Can-Eat Medford Hometown Buffet restaurant, so DeShawn and Sedale refused to lose.

The game was to 21. We were tied at 19-all when James hacked me on top from behind as I lobbed it to DeShawn for what I first thought was a game-winning jam. The dunk was waved off and I went to the line shooting two free throws for the win, since we were "in the bonus."

As I started to line up for the first free throw, a deputy entered the court and announced:

"FREEMAN, Merry Christmas! You've been bailed out."

"He can't go yet!" said Sedale.

"Yeah," added DeShawn. "He's gotta make his free throws first."

"Officer, may I make my free throws first? I've taught these kids, my kids and hundreds of others...always make your free throws and never leave the gym without making your last shot."

"Hurry it up, Freeman!" said the deputy.

"Don't choke," said Manny.

I stepped up to the line. I took three dribbles but I paused and said, "Manny, I'll make this one left-handed, for you."

"What's that shit?" said James. "Manny, we all know he's already left-handed."

Manny smirked.

The shot hit the bottom of the net as I winked at Manny. He gave me another smirk.

Then it was onto the game-winner. I dribbled three times, paused...then said..."This one's for the memory of Hank Gathers..."

And like Bo Kimble did for his fallen Loyola-Marymount teammate in the 1990 NCAA Tourney, I closed my eyes, put the ball in my off hand and shot it with extra arc. I opened my eyes just in time to hear the victorious howls of DeShawn and Sedale as the ball splashed through the net.

"Enjoy your Hometown Buffet, boyz!"

"Thanks Billy," said DeShawn as we slapped high fives, exchanged handshakes and shouts of "Merry Christmas, mofos!"

"Kill yo stalking ways," laughed Sedale. "We don't want to see your pasty white ass in here ever again."

"No prob. This was three hours more than I wanted to be in here, but thanks for helping me pass the time."

"Be sure to give Skizzle a shout to us when you're out."

"Will do, fo sho!"

I was out of my prison clothes in no time and had dressed, signed release paperwork and exited the facility. Sure enough, I had been issued with both felony and misdemeanor stalking charges. I started to ponder what this meant when I saw the most beautiful, familiar face...

It was Megan. She's one of my heroes who I had recently reconnected with from childhood. As an Internet technology specialist, she's got more brains than just about any woman

I've ever been around. She's an incredible endurance athlete. She's survived breast cancer surgery, run marathons, and let me train her en route to finishing an Ironman triathlon just last month. Training with her and her support have been a godsend. Seeing her smile as I was released from jail was like a ray of sunshine I'd never witnessed until now.

As Megs ran up and we embraced and exchanged a passionate kiss, tears flowed from her eyes as she started to speak. "I'm so sorry, Billy." said Meg. "This is all so wrong. Are you okay?"

"I think I'm going to make it, Megs. Honestly, I'm just glad I took a monster dump this morning before court. That toilet in the detainment cell was right there in the open and it sure wasn't very clean."

Megs laughed through her tears.

"Baby, please don't cry. Thank you for getting me out in time for Christmas."

"I didn't know if I was going to be able to pull it off. I thought for sure you were going to have to spend the night. Everybody moves so slow around here."

"Was Kivel and Howard helpful?"

"Yes, Billy. I spoke with Gail Vore and she told me what to do about the bail and she said you're going to need a good attorney from Southern Oregon. Billy, Downer got felony charges against you. You don't want to mess around with this one. You might have to do serious prison time if you don't get someone good to defend you."

"Megs, we'll get the bail back."

"I'm not worried about that…and Billy, you're not going to believe it, but I just had to speak my mind and I wrote out some of my feelings on my Facebook Wall and who would have guessed but in less than an hour the girls…your *Hotties*…your Facebook fans, more than ten of them, those girls wrote messages to me saying what they think Downer is trying to pull is horrible and they're going to be sending money to help with your legal costs."

"No shit, Megs. Are you kidding me?"

"Nope. Cindy, Angela, Lenora, Tammy, Kimmy, Kelly, Jennica, Karen, Connie, Pammy, Tracy, and the list goes on. You've got at least $30,000 pledged to fight her with the felony charge and so you can go forward with an appeal."

"Gotta love the Hotties."

During the past three years, I admit that I have developed quite a female following via Facebook. Some of the girls are close friends and/or others are former lovers, with whom I've been able to continue a positive relationship. Something I've learned is that every girl in this world wants to be desired. By simply stating a compliment to her, via a positive word or calling a friend one of my "Facebook Hotties," I'm been amazed at the kindness and inspiration that has been returned my way by each girl. Communicating with the Facebook Hotties is all about generating emotional responses through writing. Helping girls laugh, sigh, and cry appears to be a valid asset as noted by the response I've received from the Hotties in my time of need.

"Billy, what Diane Downer is doing is so wrong. You can rest assured that people know the truth. You are not stalking Downer. You are not violent, abusive or whatever absurd claims she wants to throw at you. The worst part of all this is how she has brought your kids down in all of this mess. Billy, you will prevail when all of this is over. I believe in you and the rest of your friends and family who *REALLY* matter, those people know the truth."

We made it back to Bend that night in time for a wonderful Christmas Day dinner with family the next day. It was great to spend a day momentarily forgetting what I'd just experienced.

But it didn't take long for Downer to reawaken me as she publicly announced her (premature) "victory." Her response sure didn't sound like someone who said, *"Your Honor, I am in fear because I think Billy will end my life."* Among her cocky expressions was an e-mail to my mom. Mom immediately forwarded it to me…

Dear Mrs. Freeman,

It's finally over. It is sad things had to go this way.

Some people just don't know when to stop. I know that Billy has a way of telling his stories and I thought you should know both sides of this one. Since you're his mother I know that you would also want to know the truth.

A Jackson County Circuit Court judge found Billy guilty today of violating a no-contact stalking order. After court the Jackson County District Attorney decided to also press charges.

Billy now faces a felony stalking charge and another felony charge for violating the stalking no-contact order.

He was arrested and booked. Lucky for him, Megan was there and bailed him out. I feel sorry for that girl though, she's being deceived, but I believe she will probably come around and some-day even apologize to me.

As a Christian, I feel that I had to put everything into God's hands and that's why I put my faith into the judicial system.

Today, justice was served.

I hope Billy can now move on. It is almost like a new life for him. When he is convicted on the felony counts he'll probably be spending at least 70 months in the state pen in Salem since I believe stalking is a Measure 11 Crime in Oregon...but, please don't quote me on this. No matter what, Billy will get to see what evil really is lurking behind prison bars.

I have attached his mug shot since I thought you might like to view it...maybe you won't though. I got it off the Jackson County inmate website before he was let go.

I thought you needed to hear my side of the story because Billy may be headed for a meltdown, and you guys are always the ones to support him.

Have a Merry Christmas.

God bless,

Diane Downer

With the e-mail letter to Mom, Downer was just heating up. As expected, she and many others piled on throughout her Facebook Wall. Downer started off the festivities on her page by posting my mug shot and the link to *The Southern Oregon Journal's* felony arrest report:

Stalking — William Blake Freeman, 47, of Portland. Ashland police Monday arrested Freeman on charges of stalking and violating a restraining order. He was lodged Friday in jail, where he was released after posting bail.

Then she really cut loose...

Let me start by quoting the Holy Scriptures...from John 7:8...
"Let those without sin, cast the first stone."
Justice is served.

No more court dates. The judge granted a (rare) LIFETIME protective order. We didn't even need to use any of our witnesses, other than the Ashland Police officer, before the judge called the hearing off!

Those of you that know me, my beliefs and what I stand for, know that spiritual forces were at work in the courtroom on Friday. I couldn't have survived this ordeal, persecution, and challenge if it weren't for Jesus! Thank God I'm a Christian. God is so good!

But just like the grace of God helped me to endure, we should have grace for Billy, who is a back-sliding Christian at best. I've always taught my kids to always shun the Devil and always turn their back on Satan and right now, I believe in my Christian heart that Billy is possessed by Satan. Tyler and Libby agree that their father needs to be put behind bars for life, or at least a long time.

I've always said that Billy needs to have his spirit broken. Maybe now this will happen and he'll turn back to God and quit running on the path of a hell-destined sinner!

We all know that my other daughter, Faith, is also speaking for the Devil, but she can still be saved. Please pray for her and while you're at it, even pray for Billy, since he will need Christ more than ever as he appears on his way to the state pen.

Thanks to all my family and friends for being there.
Rejoice and let all the praise be to Him!
God is great,
Diane

There were less than ten responses, mostly from people who are unintelligent, don't matter, or are simply unimportant. The following are the ones that seem noteworthy...at least for their emotional appeal...

(From Downer's friend, Hanna Jensen-Bowel)...

God will always take care of good people!

Praise the LORD! I normally don't do drama but Billy Freeman has disrespected my friend, Diane Downer for the last time. For his efforts, Billy Freeman finally got cuffed and stuffed! He has been harassing, stalking, bad mouthing, lying, manipulating, and victimizing poor Diane for way too many years of her life.

Billy is a crazy, rude, obsessive, STALKING FREAK! He thought he could actually get away with this but FINALLY a judge saw through his BS and had him arrested right in the courtroom.

I think it's time for a little "payback"....

Diane and I would LOVE it if all of my friends, inside or outside our church, would repost this message and let the world know that BILLY FREEMAN has finally been stopped and he's going to FRY in PRISON!

He has disrespected his ex-wife, kids, family, friends and enemies for the last time!

Please join me and pray for Billy!

Thank you Lord Jesus!

(From another one of Downer's friends, Angie "Angina" Crockford)...

God is great! Evil has been shot down...Merry Christmas Sperm Donor!

The cool part is that there was enough evidence to prove that Billy was guilty beyond a reasonable doubt so that he was immediately charged with the felony crimes.

So for everyone who has been buying into his crap, I really hope you start seeing Billy for who he really is, and be cautious about getting involved with him.

You could be playing with fire, and don't forget it can be very easy to prove that you would be an accomplice to helping him. And do you want a felony on your record? I sure as hell hope not!

I'm so proud of your kids, Diane. Tyler fought back, and while retaining the services of Mr. Fortran, Tyler was able to prove that he is a better man than his sperm donor father will ever be!

You are one class act, Tyler. Peace to you!

The best part of all this is that Billy has to now keep his mouth shut! If he goes anywhere near her or says anything publicly, his jail sentence will be extended even longer!

Go ahead Billy. Just do it! Keep telling people your sob story since we can't wait for you to be locked up for a long time!

I hope all of you have the best Christmas ever! With this great news, I know I will!

Jesus is the King of Kings and Lord of Lords!

(From Tyler James Freeman)...

Unlike some people I know, I'm not usually one to air things out in public. That's why I've kept relatively silent over the last two years. So, this is all I have to say...

GUILTY.

Dad got completely exposed. It wasn't even a close call. That's what he gets for fucking around with my mom for so long. It really is sad. But maybe now he might be feeling a bit like we all did with him airing our shit out.

All of the people that sat there and pointed the finger at my mom now look stupid. They have to admit it. There were no if, ands, or buts...

Dad was guilty. I will be praying for him as well.

Justice has been served. I hope 2011 brings peace to everyone...

Now, please quit asking me about what happened.

Happy Holidays

(And Liberty "Libby" Nicole Freeman)

The courts almost never grant these permanent orders because they are taken so seriously. If anyone thinks the decision was unfair then they are in complete denial.

According to the judge, what my dad did was proven by a "preponderance of the evidence." Unconditional love is holding people to a higher standard.

When you allow yourself to remain neutral, you take the path of least resistance. This is a huge disservice to those you love.

Mercy overcomes judgment.

Like my amazing brother said, I hope 2011 brings peace to everyone.

The saddest part of this Christmas is the bittersweet irony I'm feeling. How does a group of people, my kids and me, who were once so close, fall so far apart? How does the communication get so broken down? Believe it or not, I'm still incredibly proud of my kids. I'm even proud of Faith, for taking the stand and telling the truth. I'm proud of Tyler for sticking up for what he believes in, even though his view is a little off. I'm proud of Libby, especially with the preponderance of her vocabulary, but I'm not sure she even knows what she's trying to say, any more. I know it's a cliché, but Tyler is allowing his brain to be washed by his mother almost to the degree of poor Libby's...*Liberty Freeman*...Although Diane was apprehensive at first, she let me give our first-born the first name of "Liberty," which is one of my all-time favorite Journey songs, "LIBERTY," which most people I know can never recall hearing...

> *We all agree...*
> *We live to be free*
> *They can't tell us how to be*
> *We all agree*
> *You individually,*
> *We the people, share the power,*
> *Hold the key...*

The Monday after Christmas, word had leaked out that I was facing felony stalking charges. As a result, I was flooded by e-mails recommending good attorneys. Although I had checked on a few who were referred to me by Kivel and Howard, it didn't seem like I had the right one for the job until a familiar face came into view after a Google search for "Attorney stalking."

I couldn't believe it, but the one and only Elodie Rose Maddock was practicing law in Southern Oregon. After attending high school in Myrtle Creek, Oregon, Ms. Maddock earned a journalism degree and attended law school at the University of Oregon. After a short stint at a firm in Lake Oswego, Ms. Maddock opened her own law office in Medford. Her website was www.thestalkingattorney.com. Talk about a small world...I had first come across images of Ms. Maddock when I met an Asian girl named Malinda on an online dating service. Malinda used Elodie's photos for her dating profile. She was in a bad marriage and had borrowed the photos of Elodie Maddock off her brother's laptop since he used to date her. Malinda used Elodie's photos to cyberstalk victims including myself, but that's an entirely different story in its own right!

Anyway, Ms. Maddock's website came complete with a few photos of her (one of her dressed professionally, one running, and one—go figure—in sexy lingerie) with her background and contact info and the following statement pertaining to her crusade against falsely accused stalkers...

Fighting the Abuse of Wrongly Assigned Stalking Protective Orders

Stalking is "the act of pursuing stealthily." Stalking can be either admired, desired or against the law. Stalking can be conducted by a psychopathic killer, a romanticist, or a combination of the two. Artists, poets and songwriters could be accused of having "stalking tendencies" just as easily as rapists and arsonists and psychopathic ex-lovers. Therefore, literary geniuses can be stalkers, just as easily as convicted felons.

Nine out of ten women with relationship problems, or even women who desire a boyfriend, have the secret dream of being stalked. They crave the attention and when few or no one from the opposite sex has any attraction to them, the stalker dream races with greater intensity with each passing night these women spend alone.

In Oregon, a stalking protective order (SPO) may be obtained when a person is subjected to repeated and unwanted contact that coerces her (OR him), or causes reasonable apprehension regarding personal safety. Stalking orders are a vital tool in preventing abuse and protecting people from contact that reasonably places them in fear for their own safety.

These unwanted contacts can include crimes committed by another, such as physical harassment, following or waiting

*for a person outside school, work, home, assault, or making
serious threats of imminent personal violence.*

*To obtain a stalking order a party can simply fill out a
petition to be presented before a judge (without the other
party being notified).*

*As a result, this uncontested scenario is ripe for abuse. To
obtain a stalking order, all a person has to do is fill out a form
alleging two or more alarming contacts. Although the petition is signed under penalty of perjury and the respondent is
entitled to a hearing, there are immediate consequences to
the respondent regardless of the final outcome. First, there is
a court finding of probable cause that the respondent is a
stalker. Second, collateral consequences often occur with
employment. Many employers don't want to retain an
employee who is accused of stalking, let alone found guilty.
Third, it immediately affects a person's right to carry a concealed firearm.*

*In Jackson County, Oregon, there is a culture of people,
particularly women, who abuse stalking orders, using them
as a tool to be vindictive and get even with ex-husbands, who
discover wrongdoing after their divorce, sometimes years or
even decades after the ex-wife's transgressions come to light.
Stalking orders have been used to strike back at neighbors or
a girlfriend's ex, or for a jilted woman to even gain an advantage of taking custody of her grandchild again the grandchild's parents.*

*This sort of abuse undermines the legitimate stalking
claims. Fortunately, stalking orders are civil matters that
afford considerable opportunities for preparing for trial and
defending against frivolous claims (respondent's request that
the petitioner pay attorney fees, depositions, requests for pro-
duction, etc.).*

*I have tried many stalking order cases in court and have
argued stalking order case law before the Oregon Court of
Appeals. Challenging a stalking order requires a specific
knowledge of the relevant Oregon cases, particularly those*

cases involving protected speech (State v. Rangel) and its progeny.

Can stalking orders be made PERMANENT? Is there such a thing as a "LIFETIME" stalking order? The answers to these questions are a resounding ABSOLUTELY NO WAY!

Can permanent stalking protective orders be terminated?

The answer to this question is... ABSOLUTELY YES!

In Edwards v. Biehler in 2005, the Oregon Court of Appeals ruled that respondents subject to stalking orders of unlimited duration can now file a motion to terminate the stalking order!

Also after the stalking order is terminated, I can help you put your life back together by having the terminated order expunged and dismissed from the record of the wrongly accused.

In Jackson County alone, I have terminated and expunged hundreds of stalking cases for clients who have been wrongly accused of stalking.

I know what stalking is and I know what it is not. I know women, some who were once even personal friends, who wrongly accused their boyfriends and ex-husbands of stalking.

I am The Stalking Attorney. I am here for you. If you have been falsely accused of stalking, call me today so I can help.

Elodie Maddock

Attorney at Law

I immediately fired off a phone call to Ms. Maddock. Although she wasn't in the office, the receptionist gave me her e-mail address.

So after a couple more days, I had pulled together my story and decided to send it to Ms. Maddock. If she's going to represent me, she'd better know what she's dealing with.

Dear Ms. Elodie Maddock,
Good afternoon. You've been highly recommended.
I have a short story I'd like to share with you.

Unless I give you permission at a later time, I trust you will keep the story confidential from anybody else, including other attorneys inside (and outside) of your office.

I want you to have it up front because I've been already charged with felony crimes and I need your help.

Please let me know when you complete the attached manuscript so we can select a time/place to answer any questions you might have.

I look forward to hearing from you.
Sincerely,
William "Billy" Freeman / 503-555-1375

Ms. Maddock was quick. She replied the next day.

Mr. Freeman,
Sorry I do not have time to read your "short" 130-page story. If you really need an attorney for felony charges, I practice criminal defense and I charge a $300, one-hour initial consultation fee.
Elodie Maddock

Ms. Maddock,
I'm terribly sorry.

I thought by reading the draft of the manuscript I sent, a *"love story gone wrong, then right,"* that you'd better understand who you're about to represent.

Please understand that the story is not finished and I'm still having faith for a happy ending.

I believe that with your background, experience, and education, your maturity level would be in concurrence. If I'm mistaken, then by all means, do not read it.

My understanding is that your fee was more in the neighborhood of $400-$500 per hour. If you aren't getting compensated at that level, you might want to consult a new financial advisor. This is just my opinion, of course.

Here's something I'd like to propose...I'm sure you can drill through this document in less than two hours Therefore, I'll pay you $800 for you to carefully read it. You'll receive payment immediately after my "initial consultation," which would be included in this fee.

Otherwise, I'll have to go seek out another attorney. At this point, you're still my first choice...and by the way, I like your fire, Ms. Maddock!

I look forward to hearing from you.
Sincerely,
Billy Freeman

Respectfully,

Mr. Freeman, I will not "go ahead" and read anything without some form of retainer agreement, and you "promising" to pay me a sum after reading will not suffice.

Obviously, you do not know as much about attorneys as you would like to pretend—you have made absolutely no effort to explain how this "story" could possibly have anything to do with any sort of criminal action. As such, I do not see how I can be of help to you. I'm sorry but I will not read your "story" just because, and I certainly will not be reading it without a prior consultation and retainer agreement.

Let me ask you this—just whom do I come "highly recommended" by?

Oh, and "Mr. Freeman"—I'm not sure how you think you have an "understanding of my fees," but a consultation fee is not an hourly cost. And if you really knew anything about my practice, you would understand that we mainly work on flat-fee agreements. I surely do appreciate your insulting suggestion that I get a "new financial advisor," but after seven years of higher education I think I'm pretty "knowledgeable" in that area.

Ms. Maddock,

Now we're getting somewhere. We do agree on something—I DON'T have a CLUE regarding attorneys. I was just making a guess on what I imagined you were worth. Thank you for clearing that up.

What I do know, however, is a bit of common sense. If two people are going to work together, we're going to have to trust each other. Whether it's an attorney, stockbroker, a client, or even a friend, *TRUST* is the most important element, in my book.

Do your clients trust you? How am I supposed to trust you if you don't trust me to pay you? I mean no offense or "insults" by these questions. I'm just curious.

All right, I'm still interested in doing the consultation with you, but I want you to have some background before we meet. It took more than ten months for all of the circumstances to come to light. Is it wrong for me to assign you some homework, to get you up to speed, before we meet? If I must, I'll send you a check up front if necessary. I mean no disrespect.

With all of that Higher Ed you've received, in addition to the Bar, is it safe to conclude that you've passed the Series 7 and 66 examinations as well? If so, then congrats, Ms. Maddock. Whether you realize it yet or not, you are a true inspiration!

And besides your fire, I like your tenacity! These are the exact traits I'm looking for. I bet you'd make a great marathon runner!

Have you seen the film *Moulin Rouge* more than once? (Again) I'm just curious...

Best,

Billy Freeman... p.s. ...In good time, I will tell you the name of the person who recommended you. Right now, I think it's best for all involved if her identity remains confidential. But honestly, I think you already know her identity. There is one thing I can tell you now:

I am real...

The burning question remaining for you, Elodie Rose Maddock is...

Are you?

Here's another idea...

Elodie,

How about this? If you haven't already, just try the first three chapters. I think you might even start to understand why I sent the document to you after you allow yourself to do this. This will probably take you all of ten minutes! In fact, Chapter Two even looks like it could have been inspired by a cute girl who once attended South Umpqua High School. Imagine that? However, I'll let you be the judge.

Billy

Billy,

Why don't you find another attorney since I WILL NOT be reading your "story." This ends our communication.

Very well, Elodie

I'm waiting to hear back from another attorney as I respect your wishes to turn the page...I'm getting the feeling that you think "William B. Freeman" is a "fictional character"? That couldn't be further from the truth.

Maybe some evidence would put your mind at ease?

I'm attaching six photos. I can send more if necessary, if these aren't convincing enough.

Have a great day.

Best,

Billy... Oh...Ms. Maddock...There is one other thing...Do you by any chance know a woman named *"Malinda Yeager"*? (six photos attached)...

Mr. Freeman,

My concern comes not from your identity but rather these little "games" you continue to play through your e-mails. People who are facing criminal charges are not afraid to tell their attorney WHAT the actual criminal issue is and by WHOM they were referred. I do not have the time or patience to "go ahead and read" anything for which I have not been paid, let alone something that I believe to be some little game someone is playing. Whether I "trust" you to pay me for work done is immaterial; I am a CRIMINAL DEFENSE ATTORNEY. Many of the people for whom I work are CRIMINALS—thus I won't work until I'm paid up front. Best of luck finding an attorney in this field otherwise who is willing to work for you.

Further, I do not know how or why I fit into your game/plans, but I am working in a legitimate business here and your ridiculous actions and evasive e-mails are interfering with the time I need to be spending on my clients that actually need real help.

In good time,
Ms. Maddock

Good morning,

"Malinda Yeager" is the name of the woman who recommended you. During a number of months she sent an array of photos. Malinda said that she appears in each of the pictures. I'm attaching some of them for you to view. There are many more if necessary.

Therefore, I'm curious. Do you actually know this woman? Is each of these pictures of Malinda Yeager? Are they even the same woman? Again, "Malinda" said that every one of the pictures was of her. She attributed the different subtle appearances to her various hair styles, makeup, and a "sister named 'Carly' in a SoCal art school who uses Photoshop."

And doesn't at least one of them have a striking resemblance to you,

"Ms. Elodie Maddock"?

If you want to discuss this further, maybe now is an appropriate time to propose dinner? Of course, you're welcome to choose the location, but I was thinking somewhere in Ashland, either *Chateaulin*—or—there's always *Omar's* or *Alex's*? My schedule is open for Monday or Wednesday.

Let me know what you think and I'll try not to take up any more of your valuable time during business hours.

I'm also attaching the documents confirming the felony stalking charges against me.

Regards,

William Freeman...isn't it a crime...you know...claiming to be someone you aren't? If not, it should be!

Billy,

Why on God's green earth do you think I would *EVER* consider meeting you, let alone for dinner?

I have no idea who this "Malinda Yeager" is—apparently she is a liar and not a very good one. The photos clearly depict several different women—you clearly are either (1) a pushover, (2) a creepy liar, or (3) an idiot if you ever believed whoever sent these photos to you.

So this LOSER whom you apparently associate with is probably fat, ugly, and walking around with the self-esteem of a junkie hooker—thus why she feels the need to steal other women's photos and pretend to be them.

You obviously have issues as well, since you choose to believe and/or communicate with such a person.

I STRESS that I have NO idea how you got my information, how this "Malinda" bitch got my information, or why you continue to try to contact me. Let me make this clear—I DO NOT WANT TO MEET YOU—be it dinner, business, or happenstance.

What I do want is for you crazy fucks to stop involving me in whatever little game you are playing and stop "quoting" my name like I am a fictional person—you're the creep who got my information and contacted me.

Ms. Maddock

Farewell Ms. Maddock...

Thank you for sharing your feelings and thoughts in such an eloquent manner, yesterday.

It's now with great regret that I must rescind my offer from a week ago for you to read the document I sent you. Please delete it and all of our correspondences.

I would like to recommend a different story for you. It's called "The Lucky One" by Nicholas Sparks. Here's a quick summary...

Is there really such thing as a lucky charm? The hero of Nicholas Sparks' "The Lucky One" believes he's found one in the form of a photograph of a smiling woman he's never met, but who he comes to believe holds the key to his destiny...

I must say that you are the first criminal defense attorney I've ever reached out to and after the way you responded, I'll admit something…my faith in criminal defense attorneys has really taken a severe blow; one from which I'm not sure a full recovery is attainable. What hurts the most is that I truly believe in our American judicial system; however, I really didn't believe there were attorneys out there making judgments, prior to having all her facts straight. Now, I'm not so sure.

Laurence Durrell penned the following:

There are three things you can do for a woman…you can love her, suffer for her or turn her into literature.

I respect your opinion and vantage point concerning how you perceive Malinda Yeager, and my relationship with her. But Elodie, I don't think it's a crime when I tell you…*I loved Malinda Yeager, I suffered for her, and then (she gave me no choice so) I had to turn her into literature.*

When a person cares that deeply for someone who has become known as his *"Prototype,"* sometimes he can appear to be a little on the crazy side. And now, as I bid adieu to you, Ms. Maddock, you're leaving me no choice but to add…*I loved you, I suffered for you, and now I must turn you into literature…*

Mr. Durrell would be proud.

When I think of our connection these last seven days the question which keeps returning to me is the central theme from the movie, *Moulin Rouge*…Elodie…

"Would you choose the sitar player or the maharaja?"

No matter how much you might deny it, I know you'd be much happier with the sitar player.

You also can't deny that I have made you *think* a little bit in these previous seven days. Is that such a bad thing? Here is another small bit of advice I'd like to give you for your interactions with other people in the future…whether they're potential clients, friends, family, or even strangers in this world…this also comes from *"The Rouge"*…

"The greatest gift you will ever learn is just to love, and to be loved in return."

Goodbye, Ms. Elodie Rose Maddock. I'm sorry our timing appears to have been off. I still think we had tremendous potential.

Love,

William Freeman / 503-555-1375

Shortly thereafter, Ms. Elodie Rose Maddock called.

"My retainer for you is now $7,000 and I'll need another thousand for court costs."

"Seven thousand? Jesus, Ms. Maddock. Are you guaranteeing victory?"

"You should already know that I'm not allowed to do that."

"What's your track record, Ms. Maddock?"

"I've won more than two-thirds of my cases. I'm hitting sixty-nine percent to date."

"Sixty-nine? Ms. Maddock, that's not a very good free throw percentage."

"Yeah, maybe, but two for three is a helluva batting average."

"Seven thousand is steep, but let me do some checking. I think I can come up with the funds."

"Very well, Mr. Freeman. Remember, you have a January 20th court date coming up on the felony charges and you only have thirty days from the court date to file the appeal on the permanent stalking order. So let me know either way, right away."

"Will do, Ms. Maddock...and in the meantime, I've got something for you to ponder."

"What's that?"

"*A Novel Approach to Stalking*...do you think that would make a good book title someday?"

"Perhaps. You'll get my full attention and opinion after I get the retainer fee!"

"So when do you suggest we get together?"

"Call my office and set an appointment when you're ready to pay the retainer."

"Sounds good, Ms. Maddock."

CHAPTER 8:

A Novel Approach to Stalking

Within three days, the Facebook Hotties had dropped more than $20,000 of the pledged $30,000 into my account. I then wired the $8,000 to a trust account for Elodie Maddock which was set up in my name. I called her and scheduled an appointment for Tuesday, January 18. Ms. Maddock confirmed that she would be requesting discovery on all of the police reports and a transcript from the civil case regarding the stalking order. She told me that if Megan and I wanted to watch the Ducks on January 10 at the BCS Championship football game in Phoenix that I would need to call the court to get a trip permit.

The game was a great distraction. The Ducks donned their flashy gunmetal steel helmets, with a lime-colored Big O, and lime-blurry speed socks. The game was spectacular, tied at 19-all and destined for overtime. A fluke play resulted in an Auburn field goal at the end of regulation and the national championship just slipped out of Oregon's grasp.

After attending the football game, I arrived at Ms. Maddock's office for the first meeting.

"Mr. Freeman, I'm pleased to meet you."

"Ms. Maddock, please call me Bill or Billy."

"Okay Billy, you can also call me Elodie."

"Thanks, Elodie."

"Too bad for the Ducks, aye?"

"Yeah, we definitely gave Auburn a run for its money."

"I couldn't believe we lost on a botched play right at the end."

"Yeah, I think the refs blew the call toward the end. We should have had overtime."

"Elodie, are you talking about forward progress?"

"If I had to judge, that running back for the Tigers was stopped."

"Well, there's always another game."

"Sort of like another day in court."

"Yeah, there's always next year in football, Billy. And don't forget, everyone loses games, but like our Ducks, few change them."

She was just as smoking hot in person as I could have imagined. She was the epitome of the "sexy librarian" fantasy with long, blonde hair pulled up, business suit, heels, and black-framed glasses. Elodie Rose Maddock had to be at least 5'8", with non-stop legs. Damn, I thought. In her office were two plaques which stated "PAC-10 Women's Champion 5000 Meters" for 1997 and 1998.

"Wow! Elodie. I had no idea you were a long-distance runner."

"I spent a lot of time in Eugene at historic Hayward Field."

"What about Hendricks Park and Pre's Rock?"

"Billy, you know about Pre's Rock?"

"Oh, yeah. It's a place where visions appear! But that's also another story. Do you still run?"

"I try to get a few miles in every day. It really helps to clear my mind right before I go to court. Speaking of clearing your mind, have you thought about doing a psychological evaluation?"

"I did one about ten years ago. Just before Diane and I got divorced. She had my parents convinced that I was schizophrenic, bi-polar, neurotic, and Lord knows what else."

"Oh Jesus Christ!"

"She tried to get me to start taking Zoloft and even asked an Ashland psychiatrist to give me a psych evaluation and write me a prescription for lithium."

"Who was the psychiatrist?"

"I believe it was Dr. Knapp. Yes! Dr. Michael Knapp."

"What were the results of that test?"

"Dr. Knapp said if I relocated to Eugene to start a business, that our marriage probably wouldn't make it. But he told me, my parents, and Diane that I absolutely was *not* mentally ill."

"She must still not agree with Dr. Knapp. Did you see the e-mail she sent to Officer Vaughn Seward?" It was included in the original police report.

"I did not see it.

Officer Seward,

At the end of this message, I'm including the text message I received from Billy last week that includes threatening statements regarding his disapproval of my placing our grandson in first grade, instead of kindergarten. Did you know it's a state law that if a kid is six years old he must be placed in first grade?

I have difficulty in even passing these texts on and any others he has created, due to the untrue and disturbing comments made about me. Although I cannot allow this to keep me quiet any longer.

I don't care what anyone reads, hears, believes, or even if he does somehow write about my life in an online forum, magazine, and/or novel to publish libelous opinions about me. People can judge me by my facts.

I am done. I am done sleeping with the lights on. I am done jumping every time I hear a noise, or not making friends because I don't want to bring them into this mess. Billy is mentally unstable. Billy is dangerous at worst, damaging at best. And I want him out of my life.

I am done for myself, and I am done for my friends and my kids who for years have been affected and worried and frustrated that I won't do anything about it.

Please contact my children, Libby or Tyler, who are adults, if you have any questions. Billy says some crazy things and it may be hard to untangle them all.

If you have any doubts at all regarding the legitimacy of my complaints or fears, I know they could tell you from personal experience how he has harassed, slandered, threatened not only me, but them.

Again, Billy is mentally unstable. He needs to be committed to a mental hospital.

"What do you make of this, Elodie?"

"First, I think your ex-wife is a nutjob!"

"Thanks, Elodie Maddock. I'm starting to love you more already."

"You're welcome. But remember, I'm no psychiatrist, and that's why I want you to get another psych evaluation."

"Why is that?"

"I need a psychiatrist to confirm that you aren't mental and you're not a stalker. It will definitely help our cause."

"Why can't we just request a psych eval done on Downer so it can be proven that she's the psycho one?"

"That's not a bad idea, Billy. But remember, you're the one who's facing the charges."

"What's that going to cost me?"

"About fifteen hundred."

"Do you have a referral shrink?"

"Yeah, Dr. Abraham Freed. Call him and tell him I sent you and we need to get the test done, ASAP."

"Elodie, what if I don't pass the test?"

"Simple, then we don't use the results. We tell the D.A. that you couldn't afford the eval."

"Damn, you *are* good."

"Thank you."

"So what's next, Elodie?"

"After I get the transcript from the civil stalking hearing, then I'll be able to advise you on our strategy for the appeal. In the meantime, I believe I can get the felony charges either dropped or reduced to a misdemeanor charge."

"So after the felony charges are dropped I'll get to keep my passport to go Down Under for the Australian Ironman Triathlon in May?"

"It's not guaranteed, but based on what I'm seeing, we've got a better than average chance for you to reach your goals.

The key for you right now is to not contact Diane Downer. The longer you go without calling, texting, or e-mailing her, the better. Billy, your past record is clean. You also don't fully meet the criteria of the stalking profile."

"Stalking profile?"

"Billy Freeman, there are three types of stalkers. These include: the Predatory Stalker, the Intimacy-Seeking Stalker, and the Resentful Stalker. I don't think you're a Predatory Stalker since he is one who acts in preparation for a sexual attack. Most Predatory Stalkers have a record of prior sex crimes."

"So we can check that one off the list?"

"Yes. Next, the Intimacy-Seeking Stalker is based on the person focusing on someone whom he believes is his true love. This type of stalker believes his love is requited or returned, the other believes that even though the love is not initially returned or that it is lost, that the love will eventually be returned and/or ignited for the first time."

"I see."

"Although, maybe you were once in love with Ms. Downer, I don't believe at this precise moment that you are an Intimacy-Seeking Stalker. This type of stalker is also the rejected one. What do you think, Billy?"

"So the predatory and the intimacy types can be the spurned lovers?"

"Most definitely…there is, however, a little gray area here with the third type."

"Gray area?"

"Yeah. The third type of stalker is the Resentful Stalker. This is where we've got to be the most careful, Billy. The Resentful Stalker has behavior meant to distress and frighten the victim. This type of stalker is the most likely person who'll threaten the victim."

"Ahhh, hence, her using the 'hell to pay' comment."

"Exactly, but it doesn't take a stalking psychiatrist to figure out that all of your text messages and e-mails to her—at least the ones I've seen so far—have been severely taken out of context. Are you sure she's not having a fling with that Ashland Officer Seward?"

"You're the second person to ask that question."

"It's quite possible, Billy."

"My daughter, Faith, was thinking the same thing, right after he cuffed me. The main reason of my being fired up in all of these experiences is not because I'm obsessed, still in love, or want to reignite any 'flames' with Downer. I just wanted my grandson to not skip kindergarten and I was sticking up for the little guy and my daughter. Downer has tried to remove the grandson three times from the daughter's care during his six years on this planet. Granny Downer has a sick fantasy of raising the kid as if he were her own."

"I believe you, Billy Freeman. Now, do you have any other questions?"

"Your website says you're 'The Stalking Attorney.' Why is that?"

"I know my stuff. I rarely lose a case. I defend people accused of stalking, especially those wrongly accused."

"Have you ever been stalked?"

"As a matter of fact I have. He was either a resentful or predatory stalker, so I shot the son of a bitch."

"Killed him?"

"Deader than the deer I used to hunt in the Umpqua River Valley when I was a kid."

"Damn. I was wondering about something else. Is Facebook legally private?"

"Great question. Just recently a federal judge ruled in California that privacy settings are the key. If wall postings are set to 'private' then the comments are judged as if a person were telling his buddies in his own private locker room. If they're public, they can be used against you."

"So if Downer's attorney claimed I threatened her from something on my Facebook Wall, and the post was not meant for her eyes since the settings were private, if someone else printed the posting and gave it to her, shouldn't she not be allowed to use it as evidence against me?"

"Precisely, at least in theory. Now Billy, I have a question for you?"

"Fire away."

"For the civil case, regarding the permanent stalking order which was issued by Judge Ronski, why didn't you have an attorney defend you?"

"Well, I'd been through one of these before and I thought I could handle it. The judge in Portland threw the case out. I guess I also figured that if things didn't work out, I could always appeal."

"I see. You know if you had called me earlier, you probably would have saved a lot of time, energy and money."

"I know, Elodie. Now, I have a confession for you, and I owe you an apology for the way our relationship began."

"It's okay, Billy. No apology necessary and regarding your story, I have an apology for you."

"Nahhh," I laughed.

"When I told you I wasn't going to read your story until you retained me, I lied."

"You lied? Damn, Elodie, you attorneys are all alike. What was the point I was trying to make earlier? You know, my whole issue regarding trust?"

"I know, Billy. I guess you'll have to spank me."

"That, Ms. Maddock, can be arranged."

"Billy! Seriously, I couldn't put your story down and I must also admit that I'm finding you quite charming in person as is the main character in your book. I also didn't feel I could admit my transgression at the time of its occurrence. You would have probably lost faith and respect in me toward becoming my client. Now, I'm sorry I interrupted you, but what about your confession?"

"Okay, what I have to admit, is that...I have been stalking you."

"YEAH, right!" she laughed.

"That girl I told you about in the e-mails. Malinda Yeager. She sent me many of your pictures. She was a helluva writer and we talked for hours on the phone. But it took ten months for her to finally meet me in person."

"Ten months? She must have really captured your imagination, for you not to push for a meeting."

"She did capture my imagination and she inspired my writing. We didn't meet right away because I was busy with work, writing, and training. She was in Seattle, then L.A., and she was really busy. I fell for her voice, her thoughts her dreams inside *your* physicality."

"Wow, I'm not sure I should be flattered or freaked."

"I definitely have the potential for being a stalker, but I'd rather call myself a seeker or a romanticist."

"Where'd she get my pictures, again?"

"She said that she got them off her brother's computer."

"Did you ever meet this Malinda?"

"Yeah, she finally decided to come clean. She wasn't ever in Seattle or L.A. She was in Hillsboro."

"Dang, when you met her in person, how did you feel?"

"The whole experience was strange and surreal. But I made her a great dinner, we had wild sex which we'd both been craving and denying for months, and when we stared at the ceiling and talked during the 'afterplay,' I honestly thought I was talking to a woman who looked like you. So, I'm sorry for—at least in part—for stalking you, or at least the *image* of you. I hope you won't hold it against me?"

"Billy, it's okay. If you get out of line I'll just shoot you like I did the other stalker."

"So when are you going to let me take you to dinner?"

"Don't push your luck, Billy. If you start really stalking me this time, that might cause a conflict of interest and I'll have to withdraw my representation of you."

"Oh, Elodie, let's not go there."

"Billy, now get out of Southern Oregon so you won't cross paths with your Downer. I'll talk to you soon. Perhaps dinner might occur down the road someday?"

"Works for me. Until we meet again, Elodie. Please remember. I know what it's like to be served with a stalking citation. I was served in Portland...I wasn't served in Medford.

And sure enough, Elodie Rose Maddock knew her shit, and she sure had some pull. Shortly thereafter, thanks to her negotiations, the felony charges were disintegrated right before our eyes. I'm not sure what she did, but as I tried as hard I could, it was hard not to become enamored by her all over again...

I scheduled the psych eval with Dr. Freed for March 21, with the results to be revealed on April 4. Elodie then convinced the D.A. to set my next court hearing on April 11. She said the longer we pushed things out, the better. She also filed the appeal docs by the deadline.

The next thing I did was throw out into cyberspace a new Facebook "private" posting of my own.

Attention Freeman Children:

I'm sorry, and I hate to tell you this, but Daddy is not guilty of what the others were alleging. Sorry, Downer. Sorry Downer's friends, Hannah Jensen Bowel, and Angina Crockford.

Sometimes what you call "justice served" might be different from others' "justice served."

Either way...

Billy Freeman is not going to the state pen, or even Jackson County Jail.

CHAPTER 9:

Doctor Stalking

One of Tyler's buddies, Justin Holt, apparently hadn't gotten my message yet since I noticed his post a little later on Tyler's Facebook Wall.

Hey Ty!
I've been a little out of the loop on vacation for a while, so I just saw that shitty story about your dad on the Southern Oregon Journal's website.
Stalker Freak Billy Freeman?
Guilty as charged.
I'm sorry your family has to go through all this, Tyler. You're a bigger man than your father, and I'm proud of you for that.
Keep up the hard work in life.
Justin

"Kids" these days face challenges we couldn't even imagine twenty years ago. When one posts something on Facebook, not only can it be used in court, he might just cross paths with the person he just bashed. This is exactly what happened with Justin Holt. Within twenty-four hours of his post, I found myself on the basketball court of the Bridgeport 24-Hour Fitness Center near Lake Oswego, where I stopped prior to checking my mail and returning to Central Oregon. Not only was I a little miffed by Justin's comments, I was also perturbed because my son had just gotten engaged to Holly and I found out about it not by Tyler, not by Holly, not by

Downer or anybody else, but Justin Holt. He posted the "announcement" on his Facebook Wall...

Within fifteen minutes at the gym, I found myself playing against him. I only had to put Justin on his back on the floor twice. The normally, mild-mannered "Christian" young man came at me and shoved me back. After we finished the game, which my team won, Justin walked towards me.

"Justin, if you're going to play with men, you've got to be able to handle some defense."

"Defense, yes! But not cheap shots, Billy!" he replied.

"Young man, I don't take cheap shots on the basketball court, at least not like the ones you've been taking at me online."

"What's that supposed to mean? Are you talking about what I wrote about Tyler and Holly getting married?"

"Somewhat, but not exactly, Justin. I'm more concerned about something earlier. I just happened to have my iPhone in my gym bag so let me grab it and then let me get my quote straight."

I had him cornered since there was only one door onto the basketball court.

"First, Justin, on your info page, it claims that you're a 'Christian.' If this isn't the case any longer, would you please change that so you won't confuse me or anyone else?"

"What are you getting at, Billy?"

"'*Stalker Freak Billy Freeman. Guilty as charged.*' Remember, Justin, you're the one who once requested me as your Facebook Friend. Aren't you being judgmental here?"

"Hey look, I'm sorry," said Justin. "I admit it. That wasn't a very Christian-like thing to do."

"Justin, what you and Tyler and everybody else that's created this mess don't understand is that there's something called '*The Appeal Process.*' Ask me about it if you want, since I'd be happy to explain how it works. God forbid you'll ever have to deal with it directly but the girl you were with during your teens and twenties just might not be the one you thought she was when you end up in your thirties and forties!"

"I'm hearing you, Billy."

"Justin, Jesus Christ…You, just can't be too careful out there, son! So, why did you publicly make these comments without talking to me?"

"I'm just trying to side with Tyler. He really helped me by getting me a job."

"So, bashing his dad is your way of kissing his ass and staying in his good graces?"

"I guess I lost my head."

"Yeah, no shit. Do you know that you are the only one of Tyler's friends who publicly bashed me? Beau, Josh, Nick, Dan, Kyle, Tony, Derek, Morgan, even Alex, who kisses Tyler's ass more than you do…Not one of them bashed me. I coached all of them when they were young, they played in the three-on-three tournaments I directed, and they know what I'm really all about. What does that tell us about you, Mr. Holt?"

The sweat in Justin's eyes started flushing with tears.

"Do you think Tyler's dad is really stalking his mother?"

"No, Billy. I've seen you in this gym. You don't have a problem meeting ladies. I honestly don't see how you'd have time to stalk Diane."

"Justin, thanks. I'm not going to ask you to talk to Tyler or try to help him see my side. He needs to figure things out on his own. But remember. In my book, one is innocent until proven guilty and that includes *AFTER* the case is through the Court of Appeals."

"I mean it, Billy. I am really sorry, it won't happen again."

"No problem, Justin, and I'm sorry I just took a couple cheap shots at you on the basketball court."

"No apology needed. That was just good defense."

"Justin, there is something that maybe you can pass on to Tyler and Libby the next time you're around them. There is nothing wrong with saying 'sorry' when you realize the story you've believed for a day, week, month or maybe even years, isn't necessarily an accurate account of the events which have actually transpired."

"I'll do it, Billy. And thanks."

"Get your ass back out on the court, Justin, and always make your free throws."

"Will do, Billy. Talk to you later."

After I returned to Bend, I got an interesting e-mail from my former cellmate, Aaron Pastor:

Hey Billy,

Sorry, It took me so long to get back to you. I just got out of jail last week and it took me a while to find the CD which included my Senior Project paper.

Oh, and speaking of paper, did you see the story in the Ashland paper about Dr. Del Norte? If not, I'm including the link from the *Southern Oregon Journal* website. Things are a little blurry but I know we talked about your ex-wife working for Del Norte during your short stay in jail.

I'm attaching my essay with this message. I look forward to hearing what you think. Although the essay didn't get me through high school, maybe it will help others who are being pursued by stalkers.

Please also remember, if teachers are allowed to carry guns, kids will think twice about bringing weapons to school.

G'Day!

Aaron Pastor

I immediately read the story online from the *Southern Oregon Journal*...

The Oregon Court of Appeals ruled this month that a father is not legally at fault in a wrongful death case involving his 16-year-old daughter, who died of sudden heart arrhythmia at Ashland Community Hospital after overdosing on drugs.

Lara Hope Morningstar died in 2002. Her mother, Christina Morningstar, sued the hospital and Ashland doctor Juan Del Norte, who took care of Laura Hope on the day she was brought to the hospital. The parents divorced years earlier.

When the case finally went to trial in Jackson County Circuit Court in 2007, a jury returned a verdict that placed responsibility of the death as follows: Del Norte 60 percent, the dead teen 25 percent, and her father, David Morningstar, 15 percent.

The jury awarded $740,000 in damages. The court reduced that amount to $444,000 to account for the 40 percent of fault attributed to the teen and her father. The court entered a $444,000 judgment against Del Norte.

The teen's mother appealed, asking that her daughter and the father not be found at fault, and that the full fault be placed on Del Norte. Ashland Community Hospital and Del Norte also appealed, alleging a juror was biased against Del Norte, and that the teen was to blame for ingesting drugs and the father was to blame for not securing pills at his house and not supervising the girl at a party.

After hearing arguments in March, the Oregon Court of Appeals filed a decision on Dec. 15 that the father was not legally at fault in the wrongful death case, but that the girl and Del Norte remained at fault.

Christina Morningstar said none of the parties in the case can discuss the decision for a month while they wait to see whether that decision will be appealed.

Del Norte did not return phone calls for comment, and David Morningstar could not be reached.

According to the Court of Appeals' written decision, the teen attended an end-of-the-season party for her softball team in 2002 that was supposed to be a sleepover at a teammate's house, which turned into an unsupervised party at a local motel.

When the father found out about the unsupervised nature of the party, he contacted his daughter and told her to be home by her curfew.

When she came home late, they argued. At some point after David Morningstar went to bed, Laura Hope ingested an unknown number of pills, including leftover pills prescribed to her father that he had stored in a box in the garage.

The next morning, she was uncoordinated, incoherent and vomiting, and David Morningstar took her to the hospital. Hospital records indicate that the teen told a nurse that she had consumed alcohol, pain pills and cocaine at the party. The father's fiancée and one of the girl's friends gathered empty pill bottles and loose pills and brought them to the hospital. One of the empty pill bottles was for a drug containing acetaminophen and propoxyphene.

The teen was treated with medicine to combat narcotics in her system and for acetaminophen toxicity.

At about 5 p.m., Laura Hope died, with the cause of death listed as sudden heart arrhythmia caused by propoxyphene overdose.

Del Norte's lawyers argued that she did not die from propoxyphene poisoning, she was appropriately treated for acetaminophen poisoning and that their treatment plan was also within the standard of care for propoxyphene poisoning.

According to the Oregon Court of Appeals, Laura Hope could not be found legally at fault in the wrongful death case for taking the drugs, but she was partially at fault for not telling hospital staff what she had taken.

The Oregon Court of Appeals found that the teen's father was not legally at fault in the wrongful death case because any actions he took that may have contributed to her death happened before she was hospitalized.

Lawyers for Del Norte had argued that Laura Hope was partially at fault because two months before she died, she made a possible suicidal gesture by taking a number of unidentified pills. They said David Morningstar failed to secure prescription and non-prescription drugs in the house, and failed to supervise his daughter at the motel room softball team party.

The Jackson County Circuit Court jury had agreed with that argument in allocating 15 percent of the blame to the father. The Oregon Court of Appeals overturned that portion of the jury's verdict, placing no legal fault on the father.

The appeals court reallocated the fault for Laura Hope's death, placing 29.4 percent of the fault on the teen herself and 70.6 percent of the fault on Del Norte.

I forwarded the story to Faith and within an hour, she called.

"Dad," said Faith. "I honestly have wanted to talk to you about this for years. I have a confession."

"Okay," I replied.

"Dr. Del Norte took the hit for Mom on this one."

"Why am I not surprised, and what exactly do you mean?"

"Laura Hope didn't get the drugs from her dad. She got two bottles of painkillers from Mom and she got the cocaine from Abigail."

"Abigail Haynie? Your former stepsister?"

"Yeah, two college boys who showed up at the Bard's Inn gave Abigail the coke."

"Why did your mom give Laura Hope painkillers and why were you at the motel?"

"Mom told us we could have the sleepover at her place. Laura Hope was having major pain after she crashed with the catcher in a play at the plate during our softball game earlier in the day. Her knee was really hurting her and she was in tears, so Mom gave her a bunch of pills from her doctor samples. She had some pills she called Darvon, or they might have been Darvocet, in some unmarked bottles."

"And what about the motel?"

"At about ten, like every other night, Mom wanted to be alone to drink, smoke, read her romance novels and write in her journals. So she gave Libby her driver's license and credit card and told her to take all of the girls and the party to a motel room so she could be alone."

"So your mom rented the room on her card, with her I.D., and kicked you out so she could be by herself?"

"Exactly. After Libby got us the room, she went back home and returned Mom's credit card and license and then she went to bed."

"Wow."

"Dad, I'm telling the truth when I say that the time I saw cocaine with Matthew Fox, that was the only other time in my life I've seen it. Seeing it at the softball sleepover was the first time."

"I believe you, Faith. So you saw Abigail and Laura Hope snorting coke?"

"Yeah, after it got late. Most of our teammates left by midnight. Jenna and Ragen Bagwell were the only ones who stayed the night in the motel. At about one in the morning, after Abigail and Laura Hope took cocaine, they left with the college guys. Then the next night we got the horrible news that Laura Hope had a heart attack and died at the hospital and Juan was the on-call doctor at the E.R. when Laura Hope died."

"Why do you think none of this story came out in the investigation?"

"That night, Jenna and Ragen came by the house and Mom begged Jenna, Ragan and me to swear to Jesus and promise not to say anything about Libby getting the room for us with Mom's credit card or that she had given Laura Hope the pain pills."

"So it looks like you girls kept your promise. What about Abigail?"

"The day after Laura Hope died, Abigail's mom whisked her away to Mexico for a year on a 'foreign-exchange' program."

"Then your mom started dating Abigails's dad, Ryan, shortly thereafter."

"I know, Dad."

"And then Ryan and Abigail's mom got divorced and then Downer married Ryan. Wasn't that convenient?"

"I know, Dad."

"I thought your mom married Ryan because he had great medical insurance that would cover you when you spent that month in Portland for eating disorder treatment."

"That's what she likes to say, but really I believe she married Ryan because Abigail told him everything that really happened with Laura Hope and Mom wanted to make sure he kept his mouth shut."

"Damn, your mom has more lives than a cat."

"I know. And Dr. Del Norte has had to take the hit all of these years."

"It's shameful."

"I feel terrible, Dad. Is there anything that can be done now?"

"I don't know. I'm going to call Dr. Juan and see if he and I can set up a time to chat."

"Oh Dad, I have some other news. Erasmo and I had a parent/teacher conference yesterday with Trystan's teacher. We received his first semester grades and they are not good."

"There's another surprise."

"The school principal and Trystan's teacher are recommending that he be moved back to kindergarten immediately.

He's being placed in Mr. Lowry's kindergarten class starting tomorrow."

"They have a male kindergarten teacher at Trystan's school?"

"They do. I know it's a rarity."

"Wow, there's some good news. It's nice to know that the educators could finally figure things out. So how did you and Erasmo respond to them?"

"I told them thanks, and Erasmo said he trusted that they know what's best."

"And what does this say about your mother?"

"Dad, can we let this one go, now? Trystan is finally where he should be. I'm just happy for him."

"Okay, Faith. You're right. And a half year of kindergarten is better than nothing."

I met Dr. Juan Del Norte shortly after moving to Ashland in 1990. He became our family's doctor shortly thereafter.

The first three voicemail messages I left for Juan at Del Norte Family Practice in Ashland did not result in any returned calls. Finally, I was able to reach Susan, his step-mom, and she convinced Juan to return my call.

"Long time, no talk Dr. Juan."

"Hi Billy, how have you been?"

"I'm surviving, thank you. Hey, I'll cut right to the chase. I saw the most recent Laura Hope story. I was hoping we could get together for a beer and chat?"

"Billy, as you can imagine, the attorneys won't let me talk about it."

"Juan, I'm well aware of that. So how about we talk *OFF* the record? It's been a long time and I think it would be good for us to catch up."

"Billy, I don't think it's a good idea…and just between you and me, I've been trying to forget about the Freemans, particularly Diane, for a long time now."

"It's Downer now, Juan. She went back to her maiden name."

"Freeman, Downer, whatever. I just don't know what purpose our meeting would serve."

"How's your wife Mary and the kids?"

"They're doing great, Billy. Thanks for asking. Again, I don't see any reason for us to get together."

"How 'bout reminiscing? Don't you remember when I covered for your ass when we went to Robbie's bachelor party?"

"Billy, thanks for the offer, but I gotta run."

He hung up on me. It took me all of three minutes to decide to drive the next day to Ashland and make an "in-person" appointment at the offices of Del Norte Family Practice. One doesn't endure seventeen marathons and three Ironman triathlons without being a little persistent, stubborn and even a little pushy. Besides, I'm an "alleged stalker" so what Dr. Juan Del Norte thinks of me can't be any worse than that.

I entered the Del Norte Family Practice office at just after five p.m. The receptionist greeted me. I told her my name and that I just happened to be in the area, so I wanted to say a quick hello to Dr. Del Norte. She said he was seeing his final patient of the day, and she would let him know I was there. I took a seat in the waiting room. Within a few minutes, Juan actually greeted me with a smile.

"Billy, sorry about dropping your call yesterday."

"No prob, Juan."

"Now, what brings you here? I hope you're not stalking me."

"Oh Jesus, Juan. Now I'm *doctor stalking*. Don't tell me..."

"Yeah, I read the papers, too, Billy."

"Since you had to ask, Juan, I'm actually having a little issue with a strained Achilles."

"From running?"

"Yeah, I was hoping to squeeze a run in around Lithia Park, but the dang leg keeps flaring up."

"Shall we discuss your Achilles over a pint?"

"I was hoping you'd be able to."

"Why don't you meet me at The Standing Stone in ten minutes?"

"Excellent call, Doc."

Ten minutes later, we each took a seat at the bar of Ashland's Standing Stone Brewery.

"What are you drinking, Juan?"

"Pilot Rock Pale always works for me."

"Bartender, two pints of Pilot Rock, please, and a couple waters as well," I shouted.

After the bartender brought us our beers, I proposed a toast."

"Here's to light at the end of the tunnel. No more court dates!"

"I'm with you, Billy. No more court dates. Now, what's really on your mind?"

"Well, I've got some questions after all of these years that I hope you can answer and in return, I'd like to share some things I've just recently learned that maybe can help your cause."

"Okay Billy, fire away. I've only got about an hour. Mary's going to have dinner ready. You're welcome to join us."

"That's very kind of you to offer, Juan. Anyway, do you remember the time in the mid-nineties when I called you and told you my concern about Diane and how hard she was hitting the cigarettes?"

"It's a little foggy, but I remember it some. Wasn't that at least fifteen or sixteen years ago?"

"Yeah. Probably so. I was worried first for her health, and then for the lousy example she was setting for the kids and I'd hoped you could help me help her quit."

"I'm still not sure why you called me, Billy, I could have encouraged her, but ultimately, we both know, when people have addictions or illnesses, most times they can't be fixed or cured unless they want to get better."

"I agree. At the time you were my doctor and when my dad had had alcohol issues ten years earlier, my mom had reached out to her doctor for help with Dad, and I think that was the catalyst for helping him into recovery."

"Sometimes you can't predict things, Billy."

"Yeah, but I just always wondered why you didn't seem more willing to help with Diane?"

"I thought I did help, Billy, but if you perceive that I could have done more, then I'd like to apologize. I'm sorry."

"No sweat. What you're saying means a lot. Now, before you went out on your own, in your own office, Diane worked for you and the other three doctors at Ashland Family Care. But you guys canned her. Why did Diane get fired there?"

"I really didn't have a whole lot of say. It was mostly due to the wishes of the other three doctors and I had the least amount of seniority."

"Okay, why did the other doctors can her?"

"I promised them I wouldn't disclose those details."

"Was Diane hitting on you when both of you worked at Ashland Family Care?"

"Billy, come on."

"Juan, it's okay to admit it if she was. You wouldn't be the first one."

"Do you want another pint?"

"Sure."

"Okay, Billy, here's the story. Right after your family moved to Ashland, you know Diane started out as our receptionist, then a couple years later, I taught her how to be my medical assistant. We became quite close. We worked with a lot of patients together, helped a lot of people, and even saved a couple lives together.

"But, I will admit, when the office manager position opened up, she changed almost overnight. It was almost like she was possessed or at least under the influence of something. Then things started to get scary. I'm not kidding you…

"It was almost as if she were stalking ME!

"I kept running into her around town more frequently…grocery stores, kids' soccer games, in the ski lodge at Mount Ashland, at the Elizabethan Stage, and you and I both know how much she hates Shakespeare.

"Then, I remember it clearly as if it were yesterday. One night, about the time you had called about her cigarette smoking problem, she and I were the only two left at the office when I caught her fishing in the pharmaceutical cupboards where we kept all the drug samples.

"I asked her why she had three paper bags full of sample pills? She laughed and all of a sudden she got all lovey with me and reached over and turned up the volume on the desk radio and the next thing I knew she had asked me to slow dance with her and I had just had a really challenging day, and it was if she looked into my eyes and like a wicked witch, as she cast a spell over me and the next thing I knew we had danced into an exam room, she ripped off my clothes and then she sexually attacked me on the examination table."

"No shit?"

"Billy, no shit."

"Damn."

"Then what?"

"Even though it was against my better judgment, I pushed the other doctors hard for her to become the office manager. The others were against it at first, but one of them was about to retire and the other two were so busy that they finally caved in to my wishes.

"The affair continued for years. But Billy, I swear we never went away or anywhere special. We just had sex every once in a while at the office. When you guys got divorced, it was a lot easier for me, but my Catholic guilt was always there toward both of our families."

"So Juan...square things up with me. Why did she get canned?"

"All right, goddammit. About the time of the Laura Hope Morningstar tragedy, Dr. Dean Christopher, one of my colleagues, caught Diane walking out to her car with grocery bags full of drug samples."

"No shit, Juan?"

"Yeah. Dean hit the ceiling and came unglued. And with the Laura Hope stuff making the papers and making our office look bad, I couldn't really argue with him so we consulted the other two docs and then let her go."

"But then later, you rehired her at the new office?"

"Yeah, she pressured me that she was going to tell my wife about our affair if I didn't give her a job. I reluctantly agreed, but only on the condition that she would quit using the drugs as candy samples. I really needed her to stop doing what she did at the old office."

"I get you, Juan."

"I needed her to stop fucking with my business."

"She's good at that. We belong to a quite a club."

"Diane inevitably couldn't comply so in 2005—I think— I had to fire her myself, and that's when she moved away with her second husband, Ryan Haney, to Fresno.

"I confessed my sins to my priest and he helped me break the news to Mary. It's been an incredible battle and we're still in counseling with the kids, but I think I'm going to be able to save our marriage and my family. At first the kids hated me, but now they've been willing to sit down and talk to me and Mary and although I'm still struggling with Lucas and Paulo, our two oldest, they are breaking down walls and at least coming to the table."

"That's great news about Mary. Congrats. Now let me ask you this…If I could help you with your appeal with the Laura Hope case, would you be interested?"

"Perhaps."

"Did you know that Diane not only gave Laura Hope the pain pills, she's the one who rented the motel room for the softball team? That way Diane could perform her nightly ritual to be alone to drink, read her romance novels, write in her journal, and smoke her cigarettes."

"Billy, are you being straight with me. How did you find this out?"

"Faith confessed. She cracked. She told me after I sent her the newspaper story about you and Laura Hope. Diane convinced Faith and a couple of her friends to promise not to tell."

"Diane rented that room for those softball girls so she could be alone to smoke her cigarettes?"

"Yeah, Juan, that's what Faith says."

"Damn, Billy, maybe I should have listened closer to your call for help. Maybe I should have tried harder to help you get her off the cigarettes?"

"No shit, Dr. Del Norte. Just don't beat yourself up over it. The Downer is not worth it."

A few days later, Dr. Juan Del Norte and I got together again for a brief meeting in Portland. This time we met with his attorneys, Mick Hoffman and Steve Rasmussen, at the law firm of Hoffman Hart & Wagner.

"Mr. Freeman, for Dr. Del Norte's sake and the others involved, I wish we were having this meeting at least three years ago," said Mick. "Right now we're up against the clock with statute of limitations issues. We'll make every effort to include these new developments in the upcoming appeal. Will your daughter, Faith, be willing to testify?"

"Yes. I'm sure she will, Mick…Faith simply wants people to know the truth."

"Okay, Mr. Freeman. Thanks for your help. Do you have any questions?"

"Just one. What happens if Dr. Juan doesn't win the appeal."

"Well, then we talk about pushing for a new trial. This will of course be up to Dr. Juan, if he wants to go forward with the added effort, time, expense, and more negative publicity to his family and his practice."

"I see."

"No matter what, there's still a chance that criminal charges against Ms. Diane Downer could occur regardless, and each of you two, Billy's daughter, and others could be subpoenaed to testify when this happens."

As we left the law firm, Dr. Juan Del Norte gave me one last shout: "Billy, last week, I meant to apologize for having sex with your wife."

"No sweat, Juan. You weren't the only one."

"O, and don't forget the R.I.C.E."

"R.I.C.E.?"

"Yeah, for your Achilles. Rest, Ice, Compression, and Elevation."

"Thanks Juan."

"Sorry we forgot to talk about that as well."

"No prob, Juan."

"What about for pain?"

"Advil or Tylenol…Stay away from Darvocet. That stuff can kill—

"Stop right there Juan. I get the picture!"

CHAPTER 10:

The Appeal of Stalking

Dear Billy,

Today the transcriber assigned to your case filed the transcript. Attached is a PDF version of it. There is an amount due of $215.00, which I will pay from the funds in your client trust account.

The 15-day period following the transcript filing is called the "record settlement" period. During it, the parties have the opportunity to check the transcript for accuracy and completeness, and to move to correct or supplement it if needed. I have reviewed your transcript and it looks fine to me. But if you see any problems with it, please let me know.

The 15th day after today is March 9th, so the record in your case will settle that day. Barring requests for time extensions, I will have 49 days from the settlement date, so until April 27th, to file your Appellant's Brief. In the next few weeks I will review your entire case file—the transcript included—to determine the strength of your appeal. Once I have made that determination I will be in touch to discuss your case and to advise you on how best to proceed with your appeal.

Please feel free to contact me if you have any questions. Otherwise, I will be back in touch later.

Elodie Maddock / Attorney at Law

p.s… Could you please send me some more of your stories? I promise I won't charge you for reading them.

I sent Elodie another of my unpublished manuscripts. This time it was one that might be considered erotica, but I figured she could handle it. A few days later I got a call.

"Billy. Hi, it's Elodie."

"Hey, how's everything with my stalking attorney?"

"I've been doing some thinking and I think now would be a good time for us to get together. I'd like to talk about the stalking misdemeanor case and I think it would be good for us to get to know each other better before we go forward with your appeal of stalking."

"Elodie, you're running the show. When were you thinking?"

"I'm really slammed during the day with court and clients. How 'bout Tuesday, March 29th? I was wondering if you might be interested in going running with me in Ashland's Lithia Park? Then I thought we could do dinner and I've even got tickets to Shakespeare."

"Wow. That all sounds great, Elodie. What play are we seeing?"

"*Measure for Measure.*"

"Sounds good. Not sure I've heard of that one."

"It's one of Shakespeare's problem plays. It's billed as a comedy, but it actually shifts violently between dark, psychological drama and the straightforward comic material. The Oregon Shakespeare Festival is actually billing it as a 'tragicomedy.'"

"Tragicomedy? Wow. That sounds intense, yet potentially facetious. What's it about?"

"Ironically, it's about a sex-starved judge named Angelo who is a hard-ass when it comes to sexual immorality. He later reveals that he's hypocritical when he makes a deal to release a man he earlier convicted. In return, Angelo gets to have sex with Isabella, a virgin nun."

"Sex with a virgin nun? Damn! Leave it to the Bard!"

"Billy, I thought you'd be intrigued by this play. Especially after I read your latest erotica."

"March 29th? Okay, I'll make it work. What time?"

"I'll meet you at the Plaza in Ashland next to the Lithia water fountains. Let's say 3:30. And what size Nike running shoes do you wear?"

"See you then at 3:30. I wear size eleven-and-a-half and that's a funny question. Oh, did I tell you I'll be down in Medford on March 21st for the psych evaluation? The results are supposed to be available at my next appointment on April 4th."

"Sounds good, Billy. I might be able to get Dr. Freed to give me the results by the time we get together. He owes me a favor."

"See you on the twenty-ninth."

About a week later, I received a letter from Elodie. Though I thought it was a bit odd, she also sent a brand new pair of Nike running shoes, the Lunar Eclipse+ models in size eleven-and-a-half, with a matching Dri-Fit top, shorts and socks to go with them.

Dear Billy,
I have just received copies of your Facebook pages from the D.A.'s office. They are not helpful to our cause. Please do not continue to post things about stalkers. It looks as if you don't take this process seriously.

I told you that the D.A. believes that most stalkers have mental health issues. The purpose of your seeing Dr. Abraham Freed is to inform the D.A. that you do not fit the profile of a stalker. These Facebook pages make it much more difficult.

Please contact me when you receive this letter. I look forward to hearing from you.
Sincerely,
Elodie

I immediately called Elodie.

"Hey Elodie. Thank you for the new running gear. You shouldn't have."

"Billy, I know you've been stressing out a lot, and I wanted you to relax and work in some new shoes, prior to our getting together."

"That's great. I love the shoes. I'm going out for a run right after we get off the phone."

"Billy, I also think I know why you're posting on Facebook."

"Elodie, are you talking about the stalking pictures and cartoons."

"Yes, Billy. The D.A.'s going to be able to argue that you're wacko if you keep it up."

"Elodie, are you a Facebook friend with the D.A.?"

"No Billy, I don't do Facebook. I deal with questionable people in person all the time. I don't need to be dealing with them online as well."

"Weren't we introduced online?"

"Don't remind me, Billy. Besides, you're different. But I promised myself I wouldn't respond to anybody in the future like I did with you."

"That's probably a good idea for you. I want you to know that I'm not a Facebook friend of the D.A."

"I see, but what's your point?"

"I'm also not a Facebook friend with Downer, her two friends—Angina or Hannah—or my kids, Libby or Tyler."

"Yes?"

"So how would the D.A. obtain editorial pictures and opinionated cartoons and comments I posted in my PRIVATE Facebook locker room wall?"

"Someone must have pulled them out of your private page and sent them to him."

"Elodie. You are so good."

"Elodie… Have you Googled the words 'stalking' and 'stalker' lately?"

"No I haven't."

"Well, I have. As the stalking attorney, you know, EVERYBODY has a story to tell about stalking and stalkers. They either have a story about when they were stalked and/or a friend who once had a stalker. Stalking is becoming a cultural and societal phenomenon. There are cartoons in the editorial pages and comics sections with stalking themes almost every day."

"Billy, as I said in my letter, you need to take the court process seriously."

"I stopped posting stalking cartoons and pictures weeks ago because I was wearing out the topic."

"Billy, you just need to stop. At least until after this is over."

"Elodie, I will stop, per your request. But we have a bigger issue at stake. I have not contacted Downer since I was wrongly thrown in jail. I have not e-mailed her, called her, talked to her in person, asked others to give her messages, or followed her. Let me make things very clear, I did not send her messages directly. She should not be allowed to play 'literary critic,' and interpret my First Amendment, American Freedom of Expression, rights in HER way and be allowed to cry 'stalker' or 'stalking' to the district attorney and get away with it."

"Billy, I agree with you."

"So Elodie, how about you whip some ass and get the D.A. to dismiss the misdemeanor charge so we can focus on the appeal of the SPO?"

"I'm on it, Billy. But could you please just not make my job any more difficult?"

"Will do, Elodie. Now I just got a new pair of shoes, and I want to run."

Contrary to earlier in the winter, I enjoyed my two leisurely drives to Southern Oregon during the latter part of March. The first was on March 21st for the psych eval with Doctor Freed; the second was on March 29th. On the first trip I picked Faith and Trystan up from his kindergarten class, and we enjoyed a nice lunch at the Roadhouse Grill in Medford. Trystan loved throwing the peanut shells on the floor.

After lunch, I drove to Ashland and rented a room at the Bard's Inn. I actually knew the manager from the days of the basketball tournaments in the nineties. When I asked her how far her computer records went back, she told me she could access info from 2000. Sure enough, within minutes, I had obtained a receipt from Saturday, May 11, 2002, confirming that Downer had rented a room with her credit card for the "supervised" high school softball team party. The receipt also had Libby's handwriting for Downer's signature.

At about three p.m. I put on my running gear and ran to the Plaza in the heart of Ashland. I slowed up and walked to the Lithia water fountains. I bent over to take a swig of the natural, Lithia "seltzer" water. I immediately jumped up as someone had approached from behind and gotten close to my ear.

"You gotta be crazy to really drink that stuff," said the familiar voice.

"Damn. You almost scared me."

"*Almost* scared you?" said Elodie. "That's gotta be a first."

"Maddock, I want you to know that these magical mineral spirits are good for psych patients."

"You don't say, heh?"

"Don't knock it until you try it. The lithium in the water works wonders for the mind."

"I think I'll pass."

"I'm not kidding. Downer had my parents convinced that I had schizophrenic symptoms just before the divorce. She even asked Dr. Knapp here in Ashland to prescribe lithium for me."

"Billy, didn't you tell me this story before?"

"Of course, Maddock. Now take a swig."

I turned on the fountain for her. Damn, she was beautiful, I thought. Elodie Maddock was clad in hot pink women's Nike Lunar glide running shoes and socks, complete with matching hot pink running top and shorts. She also wore a pink-swooshed running cap with her blonde ponytail pulled through the hole in the back of the cap. She immediately spewed her water onto the sidewalk.

"Billy, it tastes like sulfur!"

"Sorry, Maddock, I guess it's an acquired taste. Shall we run?"

"Yeah, let's do it. Nice running gear, by the way."

"Thank you. Someone I know has good taste in attire."

The temperature was quite warm for this time of the year, in the low-to-mid sixties. We started running through the park and onto the trails, through the trees, grassy areas, and other foliage. "How far do you want to go?" I asked.

"Oh, three or four miles today will be good."

As we were running on the trails, there were times when the path narrowed. I let Elodie run in front a few times, and I took the lead at other times. I admit, I was struck with a funny feeling during our run, a microcosm of our brief relationship. Although we ran together side-by-side most of the time, during parts of the running experience, I felt like I was pursuing—dare I say—*stalking* her. Yet at other times, like just before we finished, she was pursuing and *stalking* me.

"Whew, good work," I said as we decided to cool down by walking the final few blocks from the Oregon Shakespeare Festival's Elizabethan Stage.

"You're a machine, Billy. You're certainly a challenge to keep up with."

"You were with me all the way."

"By the way, Billy, I don't know about that. So what time is it?"

"Just a little after four."

"I'm going to run home and get showered and changed. I've got something for you."

"What's that?"

"It's a keycard to the penthouse suite of the Ashland Springs Hotel."

"Wow, that's definitely an upgrade from the Bard's Inn."

"Doug and Becky Neuman, the owners, are good friends of mine. They take care of me."

"I know Doug and Becky. I used to play basketball with Doug all the time when I lived here. Their daughter and my daughters played softball together."

"Anyway, I also got you a massage appointment at the Waterstone Spa and our dinner reservations are at the Chateaulin Restaurant at 6:30 p.m. I'll see you about 6:25."

"I'll dash over to the Bard's Inn, grab my duffel and be right back."

Elodie took her running cap off, removed her ponytail holder and shook her long blonde mane free. DAMN, I thought. It was tough keeping my composure.

"Maddock, has anybody ever told you that you look like Marissa Miller, the former *Sports Illustrated* Swimsuit Edition cover model?"

"Once or twice, Billy. You know, when you call me by my last name, you sound just like a coach."

"Sorry, Maddock... errr... Elodie, it's an old habit."

"I think it's sort of a turn-on," she winked, then turned and jogged away.

I must admit, it seemed a little odd that my criminal defense attorney was buying me gifts and paying for massages and hooking me up with hotel suites, Shakespeare tickets, and making dinner reservations. However, it was actually sort of nice to be around a woman, whether we're working together or not, who knows how to give a goodwill gesture.

After I grabbed the duffel, I quickly made it to the top of the tallest hotel in Southern Oregon, showered, and headed down to the Waterstone Spa for my massage.

The massage knocked me out. When I came back to reality, I thought I'd just woken up from receiving nitrous from my old dentist, Doctor Zundel. I was recharged and regenerated for the night. I only had a few minutes to clean up and get downstairs and down the street to the Chateaulin. I dressed in black slacks, with a matching black velvet long-sleeved shirt and black leather shoes.

At 6:15 I was walking in the hotel lobby when I crossed paths with a familiar face. It was Doug, the owner. Although we hadn't seen each other in at least five years, he hadn't changed a bit; about 6'1", muscular, mustache, wearing basketball gear, and an ear-to-ear smile. We recognized each other immediately.

"Billy, what's up? What are you doing here?"

"Just spending the night at your house. Got dinner and drinks at Chateaulin and Shakespeare thereafter."

"Are you still playing basketball?"

"I'm retired for now. Focusing on triathlons. How 'bout you?"

"We still play every Tuesday. I had to drop by to pick up a package and I'm heading over to the Lincoln School gym right now. Next time you're in town, you should come out of *retirement* and join us."

"I just might do that, Doug. Thanks for the invite."

"Sure. Hey, I was wondering how did that three-on-three tournament with the Trail Blazers turn out?"

"Great question. That's quite a story in itself. We got it started but then ended up giving the tourney back to the Blazers. They call it the *Blazer Street Jam* now. It hasn't grown like I envisioned. However, it's well-run and I played in it about four or five years ago with Tyler and Faith. Damn near won the coed division. Other than on Christmas Eve in Medford, that's the only other time I've played three-on-three since almost a decade ago in Ashland."

"Sounds like you did a good job getting the Blazer Jam started, Billy, if it's still going on today."

"Perhaps."

"There is something I've wanted to tell you for a long time now. I never did apologize to you, Billy."

"Apologize, for what?"

"You know…back in 2002. I really wanted to invest in your three-on-three dream. But as we discussed, my investment partner had some creative issues of his own which the feds didn't look too kindly upon so they froze my assets. Anyway, I'm sorry things didn't work out for us. I think your ideas at the time had global appeal."

"Doug, no problem. You don't need to apologize. Sometimes the ball just doesn't go in the hole for you like you thought it would…or could. I'll see you on the court, another day."

"I look forward to it."

"And don't forget to keep your follow-through up."

"Sure thing, Billy."

I walked out of the lobby and turned and walked about two blocks to the Chateaulin, Ashland's finest French dining experience. I entered the restaurant and was greeted by the hostess.

"Welcome to Chateaulin. Do you have a reservation?"

"Yes, for two. It should be under Elodie Maddock."

"Here it is. For 6:30. Oh, Ms. Maddock is already waiting for you."

The hostess led me to the table. Elodie looked stunning. Her hair flowed over her shoulders and down her back, while also framing her face perfectly. Her black silk dress followed her curves perfectly, hugging her ample breasts as if she were straight out of a movie.

As we began to embrace, it also seemed only natural to give my attorney a welcoming, friendly kiss on the lips.

When we pulled apart, we each caught our breath before she said...

"Hello, William, you look amazing."

"Elodie, I was going to say the same thing to you, and what's that amazing perfume you're wearing?"

"It's called *Infatuation*."

"Wow!"

"I was going to ask about your heavenly cologne?"

"It's *ESCAPE*."

"I love it."

We sat down next to each other, as the waiter introduced himself as "Pierre." He left the wine list and the menu. Since Shakespeare started at eight sharp, we got right after it.

I suggested a bottle of the 2008 Domain Michel Lafarge Volne to get us started—a superb French Bordeaux blend red wine.

"Billy, that sounds like a wonderful selection."

Our appetites dictated that we would share the meal. We sat next to each other in the candlelight and started with the wine and appetizers including the Moules au Poivre, black peppered smoked Penn Cove mussels served with lemon and

Mignonette along with the Huitres sur la Cocue, or six oysters on a half shell.

"So tell me, what's your attraction to Shakespeare?"

"Good question, William. I love how one can compare the themes in his plays and apply them to modern times."

"Give me an example, my stalking attorney!"

"Okay...let's take *stalking* for instance. I think Shakespeare himself was a stalker. He was stalking a girl named Viola."

"Hah!" I laughed. "I saw *Shakespeare in Love* on DVD. But that was a movie with Gwyneth Paltrow, not a play."

"It was a great movie. It won the Oscar."

"Yeah, but it edged out *Saving Private Ryan*. That's still a tough call in my book."

"Well, the obvious example from a play is Romeo stalking Juliet."

"*Oh to be a glove upon her hand*?"

"Exactly. Romeo is one of the world's greatest stalkers ever. And don't get me started on Othello."

"*I will kill thee, and love thee after*?"

"Yes! And let's not leave out Lady Macbeth!"

"Why not? You're on fire. Go baby, go baby."

"Lady Macbeth was stalking the power of the throne. She used sex: sex as a weapon, the promise of it, and the denial of it to control her husband into murdering King Duncan and numerous others so she and her husband could take over the throne."

Next up was the soup and salad. The *salad maison* included Mesclun greens tossed with Trium Verjus Vinaigrette, toasted pecans and Bucheron Chevre. Our dining experience certainly would not be fulfilling without Chateaulin's world-renowned soupe du jour, French onion soup.

"Isn't this soup spectacular?" said Elodie.

"It's *Spectacular Spectacular!*"

"Oh no, not more quotes form *Moulin Rouge*, again? Billy, that's one of my favorite movies. When you quoted the

Rouge in your original e-mails you had me. That was hypnotic."

"I'm just grateful that you're representing me."

"We should talk about your psych evaluation. How did you think it went last week?"

"I thought it went perfectly fine. To me, it was like a four-hour job interview and I've usually had success with those."

"Well you'll find out for sure, directly from Dr. Freed on April 4th. But in the spirit of research and preparation, and since you gave him permission to release the results to me, I took the liberty of going over the results with Dr. Freed himself, today."

"That's fine, Elodie. What did you find out?"

"He thinks you're nuts, but it's because you do Ironman triathlons, and not because you have a mental illness. Actually, Dr. Freed thinks that anybody who tries to move his body 140.6 miles in less than seventeen hours is fucking crazy."

"No kidding?"

"Of course. Most professionals in the psychology world believe that endurance athletes are all para-suicidal, like cutters! They want to kill themselves. Marathoners, triathletes, and ultramarathoners all have a death wish!"

"Dr. Freed really believes that?"

"Yeah, but as far as your being a stalker or someone who has stalking tendencies, you're just a typical pushy, stubborn, overbearing salesman at worst, a modern Don Quixote, a quintessential Man of La Mancha at best! Your ex-wife is the one who's fucked up. No surprise here but Dr. Freed suspects she's got Borderline Personality Disorder, but he'd have to do a psych evaluation on her in order to confirm."

"Wow, really? BPD? I've heard that one before."

"Billy, her mental capacity is stuck at the age she was sexually molested…probably somewhere between ages seven and ten."…

"Damn, I thought it might be a little older than that."

"Billy, in fact, Dr. Freed has even met her before. They

were introduced at a meet-and-greet social function years ago for Dr. Del Norte. Dr. Freed said that Downer was pretty hammered and she tried to hit on him. Of course, this last part is all off the record."

"Damn, of course."

"Billy, the bottom line is that you are not stalking Diane Downer and you are not a stalker."

"No shit. Only cost me fifteen hundred to clear that up, plus your fees and the court costs."

"Yeah, but it was money well spent and I think we'll be able to go after her for reimbursement after all of this is over."

"Really, Maddock? That's good."

"It is good. And if she doesn't seek help immediately, she's on her way to having a mental breakdown."

"Elodie, I've been predicting this all along. It really saddens me for the kids and the grandkids."

Pierre then brought our main course. We'd agreed upon the Filet Mignon Bordelaise, a Snake River Farms American Wagyu beef tenderloin with Parisienne Gnocchi. It was braised with spinach and caramelized onions, Crème Fraiche and Bordelaise sauce.

"The dinner is incredible," I said.

"The cuisine is certainly delish, and I'm enjoying the company and the stimulating conversation."

"That makes two of us."

"Billy, I'd like to now advise you that we put off the misdemeanor stalking court date until sometime in May, after you get back from your triathlon in Australia."

"Works for me."

"With the positive results from your psych eval, and the additional time, I'm confident we can get a full dismissal for not only the misdemeanor stalking charge but also your appeal of the stalking protective order as well. But you have to fully promise me one thing, Billy?"

"What's that, Ms. Maddock?"

"I've already told you. Quit expressing yourself on the Internet."

"Oops. I guess I slipped and let a couple more squeeze through."

"Stop posting those editorial cartoons with a stalker or stalking theme. The D.A. is still watching. No more Stalker Kitty pictures, no more attending Stalkers Anonymous cartoons or comics about how Santa Claus is a stalker because 'He knows when you are sleeping and he knows when you're awake' crap like that."

"All right, Elodie."

"Billy, the only thing that can muck up your being cleared is if you keep pulling your editorializing shenanigans. The D.A. thinks you don't take this process seriously."

"So what's our understanding now about the First Amendment and Freedom of Expression?"

"Billy, your private Facebook locker room wall is really public in the eyes of the law. To be blunt, there are hidden cameras in your locker room and the First Amendment is fucked in this situation."

"I'm just trying to get my message across to the kids about their mother."

"Billy! Listen to me once and for all. It doesn't matter if your ex-wife is a fat fucking crazy cunt whore bitch. You can't try to communicate that message in any way, shape or form to your kids. Their mother is their mother, for chrissakes, and no matter how mentally fucked up she is, the kids will always defend her. You just have to come to terms that some people are just damaged beyond repair."

"Wow, Elodie! Have I ever seen you this fired up?!!!"

"No, but we're so close to winning this case, and I don't want you to screw this up."

"Okay, I won't. I mean it this time. I'm totally done. Oh, I also meant to tell you, my grandson Trystan was placed back into kindergarten by his teacher and the school principal. He was bombing, completely failing the first grade."

"So you were right. I get that. What you have to do now is just remind yourself that you are only the boss of you. They don't have to listen to your opinions and you've got to rise

above that. I know how it is. I'm one of the worst people in
the world. When I am right, I let people know and I am
unbending."

"That's what I like about you, Maddock."

"Yeah, thanks. I can also put both feet behind my head
and walk on my hands. Yoga will do that for you."

"I want to see that some day."

"Sure. Now, worst case scenario is if you drop the online
nonsense, I know the D.A. will at least drop all criminal
charges and reduce everything to a civil violation."

"Civil violation?"

"You'll just have to pay a fine, and the good news is if you
ever apply for a job, and you're asked if you have had any
criminal charges ever filed against you, then you get to
answer 'No!'"

"Wonderful. That's great news."

"But I'm still going to fight for you for full dismissal of
all charges."

"That's my Elodie, and you think you can win the appeal
as well?"

"I'm confident that I can argue that Judge Ronski should
not have allowed the hearing on Christmas Eve to go forward,
with you representing yourself, without first warning you of
the risks of self-representation."

"Tell me more."

"Since the judge did not warn you of those risks, the
stalking protective order should be vacated and if Downer
wants it restored, the judge should hold a new hearing. At that
hearing, I will clean her clock by contesting all of her tam-
pered, altered and fabricated evidence."

"Damn, Elodie. That would be great."

"Just make sure you get a travel permit from the court for
your trip Down Under."

"I will do it first thing tomorrow."

"And make sure there's one thing you don't do after you
leave."

"What's that?"

"Don't be marrying any Aussies goddesses while you're there and think you can stay, because you can't."

"Hey, you and I both know that just because you marry someone from another country while you're in their country, it doesn't mean that you're automatically no longer an illegal alien."

We laughed as I poured us each another glass of wine.

"Most importantly, Elodie Rose Maddock, remember...

"(The) best men are molded out of faults,
And, for the most, become much more the better
For being a little bad."

"That's *Measure for Measure*, Billy. I can't tell you how impressed I am with your wit and intellect."

"I've read the play three times since you said we had tickets."

"It's my favorite Shakespeare play, and it doesn't get its due like many of the other ones."

"Are you sure you told me that *Measure* is your favorite?"

"I'm sure."

"I *am* sure you told me that *'good counselors lack no clients'.*"

"Oh Billy Freeman, you are on a roll."

We *were* on such a roll that we even ordered dessert with a piece of the Opera Cake, a decadent layer cake of delicate almond biscuit, coffee butter cream, and dark chocolate Ganache. After we finished the cake, I looked down at my watch and realized that the show would begin in ten minutes. I quickly paid the bill and thought about how at the Oregon Shakespeare Festival, if you're five seconds late, you are screwed since the ushers won't let you in.

"We'd better get running Maddock. The show's going to start soon."

"I'm ready."

Elodie took my hand as we walked to the Angus Bowmer indoor theatre.

"It's warm enough out. I bet we could have done it outside, tonight."

"Elodie, is that a vague pronoun reference?"

"Huh, oh the play, the play is the thing. It's warm enough it could be done outside tonight."

"We'll just have to do it again after the *Feast of Will* in June."

Measure for Measure fully lived up to its billing and for its dark nature and message, the play had a happy ending. Three lines really hit home to me, some great food for thought including:

The law hath not been dead, though it hath slept.

Some rise by sin, and some by virtue fall.

Our doubts are traitors,
And make us lose the good we oft might win
By fearing to attempt

We walked out of the theatre as we had entered—hand in hand, amongst our laughter. I wasn't sure where things were going next until Elodie spoke up...

"I ordered us a bottle of Dom Perignon delivered to the room. After receiving the great news from Dr. Freed, I believe a celebration is in order."

Jesus, I thought. I think I'm starting to find out why her nickname is the "Stalking Attorney."

"Sure," I said with deep breaths, through some minimal ambivalence.

When we entered the room, as I unleashed the cork on the champagne, Elodie instantly unleashed herself from her black dress.

Damn, I thought. Elodie Maddock could have been straight out of Victoria's Secret. In fact, all she had on was a V.S. hot pink leopard-print bra and matching thong. It was a battle within for me to keep making eye contact.

"Here, Billy, I'll turn on some music and then let me help you get out of your clothes."

She turned on her iPhone which she'd hooked up to some portable speakers. She was pulling out all the stops as Barry White blasted his hit, "It's Ecstasy When You Lay Down Next to Me." Elodie handed me my glass of champagne, took hers, and lifted it toward me.

"I'd like to propose a toast. Here's to Billy Freeman. He is not a stalker."

"Thanks, Maddock."

We clinked the bottles together, looked deeply into each other's eyes, and consumed the bubbly.

A few moments later we began dancing to more Barry; this time it was "Your Sweetness is My Weakness."

Although in my past, I would have cut loose and gone crazy naked and had wild cheetah sex with a beautiful woman like this, I kept having thoughts about the "code." We are working together, I thought. I've never have had sex with ANYBODY who was ever a colleague or working for me. I had heard just too many horror stories about how these situations turned into disasters.

The next thing I knew, I was turning Barry White down.

"Elodie, I have something I need to say."

"Oh Billy, I'm just so turned on right now."

"Okay...*Condemn the fault and not the actor of it.*"

"More *Measure for Measure*. You aren't of this world. You aren't real."

"*Is this her fault or mine? The tempter or the tempted, who sins the most?*"

"Billy, you're leaving one out."

"Which one is that?"

"*Most dangerous*
Is the temptation that doth goad us on
To sin in loving virtue; never could the prostitute
With all her double vigor, art and nature,
Once stir my temper."

"Oh my! Today has been a dream—the running with each other, the massage, the room, dinner, dessert, drama, and now this. Do you know how much I'd love to make love with you right now?"

"So what's holding you back? *What's mine is yours.*"

"I have tremendous respect for you and our working relationship. And honestly, I need to run things by Megan. She's been through all of this with me all the way. And besides, we're training partners. I really should run things by her first."

"Maybe she'd want to join us, next time?"

"Elodie, I think that's a splendid idea. She just might. And I have so much love for both of you. First and foremost, you are incredible friends to me and we all have so much in common. I never want to lose that."

"I want you, Billy. But I know that we should wait, at least until your name is fully cleared by the justice system."

"What are friends for?"

"*Virtue is bold, and goodness never fearful.*"

"Do you think it would be okay with Megan if you just held me tonight, with no sex?"

"I think she'd be okay with that. I'd call her, but it's late and she's probably already asleep."

"You know, Billy, it can be lonely at times being the stalking attorney."

"I can only imagine, and I think Hamlet said it best, *Though this be madness, yet there is a method to it.*"

"Did you memorize Shakespeare from being a high school teacher?"

"A goodly bit of it, I guess."

"Goodnight, Billy, and you know something else? Hamlet was a stalker."

"Goodnight Maddock. I thought he was just crazy… because of love."

We held each other that night in the wonderful friendship we'd created, drifting off into a dreamy bliss.

CHAPTER 11:

Stalking the Stalker

The process of the psychological evaluation with Dr. Freed had flowed exactly how Elodie said. After being run through a series of mental challenges including puzzles, word association, vocabulary, 743 true/false mental questions followed by an interview, Dr. Freed confirmed in his report that I was not stalking Downer. He did indicate that I had some "potential" for developing stalking tendencies.

On Friday, April 8th, Meg and I made the journey with her three kids from Bend to Portland. The Lakers were in town to play the Trail Blazers at the Rose Garden. My dad's best friend, Buck Sherwood, had landed us a suite and four mid-court seats about three rows up to celebrate Dad's 71st birthday with a surprise party. My brother Tim, and his wife, Brooke, flew in from the Bay Area with their baby girl. Brother Steve and his wife Melissa also joined us with their two kids from Bend. My sister Cassie flew in from Reno, where she works as a high school counselor. Brother John and his wife Suzie came over. Faith flew in from Medford with Trystan. Elodie joined us, as did Dad's friends Bill Usher, Dale Andrich, and Mike and Judy Farley. Dad's sisters, my aunts Judy and Terry, were also in attendance as were Uncle Mike, cousins Stacey, Ali, Corey, and Corey's girl, Susan. It was kind of a family reunion. I had invited Libby and Tyler via text message, but knew it would take an Act of

God for them to show up to join their grandfather's pre-game celebration.

Meg and I transferred her kids to Steve and Melissa in front of the Rose Garden. Then, Meg and I met Mom and Dad at their hotel, just a few blocks from the Rose Garden, to walk them to the arena.

When we got Mom and Dad inside the Rose Garden suite, Buck turned on the lights and everybody yelled "SUR-PRISE!"

I hadn't seen Dad smile this wide since he'd made a forty-foot put to win the Elks Club golf tournament in John Day, Oregon years ago!

Dad had no idea we would all be there. We all enjoyed a delicious buffet dinner on the Lexus Club section. We finished it up with a "Happy Birthday Eddy Freeman" German chocolate cake, Dad's favorite. Everyone had such a great time in the pre-game that no one seemed to want to leave the suite. We had four seats near the floor and so by the middle of the third quarter I decided someone needed to not let those seats go to waste.

The dynamics of the game were interesting. Although Los Angeles came into Portland riding a three-game losing streak, the Lakers had defeated Portland in all three of the teams' head-to-head matchups this year. The Trail Blazers did not want to fall in the Western Conference standings, nor did they want to finish the year 0-4 against the team which could very well become their first-round opponent in the upcoming NBA playoffs.

With 3:33 to go in the third quarter, Portland had clearly taken command of the night's contest by blasting out to a 24-point lead, 74-50.

"Megs, I bet someone here will keep an eye on the kids. How about you, Elodie, Cass and I go sit down by the court for the fourth quarter?"

"That works for me, Billy."

"Elodie, Cass...come join Megs and me down by the court."

We hadn't been seated for more than a few minutes into the final quarter, when I got a strange feeling that I was being watched.

"Megs, Elodie, Cass! Keep your eye out for Tyler. I'm sure he's here, somewhere."

Meg and Elodie sat down on each side of me while Cass sat on the other side of Meg.

"How are we supposed to see him in the middle of 20,000 screaming Blazers' fans?" asked Elodie.

"Good question," I said. "He's actually not the one I'm worried about."

"Who are you worried about?" asked Meg.

"Oh shit," I said.

"Who's that in the Greg Oden jersey walking this way?" asked Elodie.

I couldn't believe what I was seeing. It was Downer! And she was acting as if she knew where we were going to be sitting.

"I'm going back to the suite," said Cass. "I don't want any problems."

As Cass darted up the aisle, I put both arms around the other two and pulled them in closely. "Megs, Elodie. Don't you two run off right now."

"Oh, I'm not going anywhere," said Meg.

"Billy. Why the hell is that crazy bitch coming this way?" Elodie added. "It's like she's pursuing you."

Jesus, I thought. I still have a stalking protective order against me and I can't even watch a goddamn Blazer game.

By that time there were just three minutes remaining when Downer reached us. She sat right down in Cass's seat as if she owned the place.

"Billy, what are you doing here?" asked Downer.

"I was going to ask you the same thing," I replied.

"You think you're Mr. Big Shot with your appeal of the felony stalking charges with your high-powered attorney, and Megan, your I.T. girlfriend, and all of the Facebook Hottie followers."

"Diane, I think you should leave."

"*I* should leave. Who invited you to this game?"

"Actually, it's Dad's birthday."

"Hell, I know that. Tyler and Libby were invited. Why wasn't I?"

"Diane, have you been drinking tonight?"

"I had a little glass of wine. What's wrong with that?"

"Do you have a ride home?"

"Of course. I'm here with Tyler and Libby."

"TWO MINUTES, TWO MINUTES IN THE GAME," said the public address announcer.

"Billy, I think you should leave. You're not supposed to be within a hundred-and-fifty feet of me."

"What? Do I need an usher to remove you from my sister's seat?"

"Billy, I think you should go," said Meg.

"She's right, Billy. You don't want to jeopardize our appeal," said Elodie.

"Billy! I'm calling 9-1-1! You're not supposed to be in the same room with me!"

"Diane. This isn't a room. We're in the fucking Rose Garden."

"Billy, I think I see Tyler on his way over now," said Meg.

Sure enough, there was my boy, 6'3", young, muscular, handsome, yet the purest momma's boy one could ever imagine.

"What are you doing, Diane? It seems like you're stalking me this time."

"Maybe I am, but it just doesn't matter does it? The law always sides with the woman. A man has to be famous—like Brad Pitt or David Letterman, if he wants to cry 'STALKER.'"

"Huh, Diane, have you lost your mind?"

"Billy Freeman, I hate to tell you this but you aren't famous!"

She began punching digits on her phone. It didn't take long to figure out that Downer had the 9-1-1 dispatcher on the line.

"I'm at the Rose Garden seated four rows up on at center court on the north side. My ex-husband is here and there's a no-contact order and a permanent lifetime stalking order against him and he's already been in jail once and he needs to go back again."

As expected, the Lakers had made a run, cutting the lead in half, to 89-77, with 1:14 in the contest.

"I'm outta here, Megs and Elodie. I'll meet you out front by the flames."

I made a dash for the aisle and toward the door. By then, Tyler was just a few rows behind me and he was hot on my trail. I got to the tunnel and then headed for the outside doors.

I could hear Brian Wheeler announce the contest via the lobby speakers and on the outside speakers. After Ron Artest hit a jumper and a free throw for the Lakers, Portland's LaMarcus Aldridge added a pair of free throws down the stretch. Derek Fisher drained two three-pointers for L.A., but it was all for naught as Portland held on for the 93-87 victory. The 20,000+ faithful erupted in a frenzy since it's always nice to smack the defending world champion (and hated) Lakers!

The celebration flowed out of the Rose Garden and into the Rose Quarter; the blazing torches in the front of the arena shot flames skyward. Just as I paused to catch my breath, I felt two arms wrapping around my legs; tackling me to the ground. I immediately freed myself and scrambled to my feet.

"Jesus, what's going on?" I knew it had to be Tyler. It was.

"Why were you following Mom at the game?"

"Son, are you back to smoking pot?"

"Dad, the cops are taking you in for good this time."

"Son, I didn't want to kick your ass in Medford and I don't want to kick your ass in Portland."

At that point we had pulled ourselves up off the ground. I could see Diane approaching, followed by Libby, Megs, and Elodie.

"Mom, don't call the cops," Tyler said as he tossed his coat to his mom.

I pulled off my sweatshirt and pitched it to Megan.

"Okay, Son, let's go."

We both put up our fists, bent our knees, starting to bob our shoulders, while sizing each other up. We started to sway in unison.

"Remember, Son, your name is Tyler Freeman, not Tyler Durden."

"Huh? Who's Tyler Durden?"

"Oh, Sonshine, didn't I teach you anything? Come on, Palahniuk?"

"Palahniuk?"

"Yeah, the writer from Portland."

"Oh yeah, *Fight Club!*"

"Don't beat up my son, Billy!" interjected Downer.

"Diane, please shut the fuck up."

"Dad, don't be talking to my mom like that."

"At least we're talking, Son. I'll take whatever you'll give me."

"Dad, shut the fuck up yourself and just fight. We can talk later."

"I'm sorry, Kobe stunk tonight, Tyler."

"Don't be ripping Kobe, he's the MVP."

"That's four losses in a row for the Lakers. If they're not careful, Portland will punk them in the first round."

"No way!"

"What was Kobe tonight, ten for thirty shooting?"

"Dad, now you're really pissing me off. He was ten for twenty-five."

Kobe has always been Tyler's favorite, ever since I took him to the Great Western Forum in 1997. Bashing Kobe seemed to provoke Tyler even more, as he came after me with raging fury. I avoided his first two punches but I wasn't so lucky on the third one.

It was a straight shot right between my eyes, but I still somehow reacted with two quick right jabs to Tyler's face, followed by a solid left hook to his ribs.

Tyler winced for a moment but immediately retaliated with a fury of punches.

Things quickly seemed to be moving now in slow motion, but it felt good, like both of us were trying to release our anger once and for all on the other.

Every punch I threw from that moment on had purpose. His mother did not have his best interests at heart. I wouldn't question whether or not she loved him; I just knew she loved herself more.

"TYLER! YOU NEED TO BEAT THE HELL OUT OF HIM!" she wailed. "YOUR DAD IS POSSESSED! BREAK HIS SPIRIT!"

The last punch Tyler landed stung me good, when my jaw made contact with his knuckles. I heard a crunching sound, like crackling potato chips, as he caught me hard on the left side of the face with a right cross. With that blow, I knew I'd probably need to swing by the hospital, but regardless of the severity of his final punch, and that fact that my face was slightly bloodied, I was still standing. The blood I was tasting within, was ironically sweet.

Next, something odd occurred which I wasn't expecting. My son stopped fighting me and asked me a question. "Dad, isn't right here where we're standing...isn't this where we played outdoor three-on-three at the Blazer Street Jam? Right here?"

"We made the coed division championship game with Faith."

"I know, Dad, but we lost that game 'cause you didn't make your fucking free throws."

"I must have made some of them that day? Not like Kobe. He missed all of his tonight!"

Tyler then launched into a machine-gun barrage of blows raining down all over me. I couldn't remember the exact three-on-three game he was referring to. The thought stunned me more than any of his punches. I rarely miss my free throws. And as that thought lingered for a moment, I was brought back to reality as someone in the crowd shouted "COPS!"

Two of Portland's finest swam their way through the crowd, breaking Tyler and me apart. It was at that precise moment that the entire crowd circled around us came into focus. All of our family and friends and even all the little kids were watching us fight. Finally, it seemed like Tyler had had enough as he turned and looked at his mother.

"Mom, I don't need to beat up Dad verbally, physically or even in court any longer. He can take all the punches we throw at him and yet he still seems to stay positive."

I smiled and winked at Tyler as the cops broke into the middle of the pack.

"What's going on here?" asked one burly Portland police officer.

As I was about to respond to Tyler and answer the officer, Downer threw herself in the middle of the police and shrieked, "Officer, this is my ex-husband. He's trying to beat up my son. There's a no-contact order. I have a permanent lifetime stalking order against him. He followed us here, he's still stalking me, and he threw the first punch."

"Officer!" shouted Meg, "This woman never tells the truth. He's not stalking her and NEITHER of them threw the first punch!"

"I'm an attorney," interjected Elodie, "and what Ms. Downer is claiming isn't what I just witnessed."

Then Dad spoke up. "Officers, I'm Ed Freeman, Tyler's grandfather and Billy's father. I'm sorry to say, but it's true. His mother has a hard time telling the truth."

The cops shot a confusing look into each other's eyes.

"All right," said the burly cop. "I suggest all of you get out of here. We've got more important things to deal with than unfounded family feuds. If you're going to fight, do it somewhere out of sight on your own property. We could nail both of you with Measure 11 assault charges and I don't think your family deserves this. Why don't you all go somewhere, like a nearby restaurant conference room, and just talk things out? Maybe you could try to solve some of your problems when you do."

"Okay," I said as I continued tasting blood as it dripped from my mouth. "Why don't we meet at Red Robin for unlimited fries and post-game milkshakes?"

"Fuck you, Dad. Not now."

Just then, Mom chimed in. "Billy, Tyler, you and your dad need to think of all the little kids. What about Trystan? He doesn't need to see his uncle fighting his grandpa, and if you two use the F-word again I'm going to wash—"

"Sorry, Grandma," Tyler interrupted. "Dad's been asking for this for quite some time."

"Sorry, Mom," I said.

"Now, I want you two to shake hands and apologize. Tyler, it's your grandpa's birthday for crying out loud! After all your Grandpa and I have done for you, the least you can do is listen to your Grandma!"

"You're right. Okay, Grandma, and happy birthday, Grandpa."

Tyler and I shook hands, as requested. I took things one step further. I pulled Tyler over to me and even though I felt sore all over, I reached my arms around my son, hugged him and said, "That was a helluva fight, Sonshine. Your dad is proud of you."

"Thanks Dad. We should have knocked the shit out of each other a whole lot sooner. Can we do it again, sometime?"

"Son, my sparring days are over and like Tonya Harding once told Dan Patrick, 'Don't make a *skeptical* (sic) out of my boxing career.' As of right now, Billy Freeman is retiring from fighting."

"It's a good thing. Some of your punches were thrown like a girl."

"Careful."

"One more thing, Dad. I'm expanding my business."

"Really? Where? To Central Oregon?"

"No, actually to Ohio. I'm moving there right after Easter."

"Ohio? Son, that's great. So who are you hiring, this time? Errrr...scratch that one from the record."

"Dad, don't even start. I learned my lesson. This time I'm on my own. Not hiring any family members, at least females. Holly and I got engaged and she'll join me out there in a month or so. And she doesn't want to work for me anyway."

"That's good. You *are* learning."

"Maybe you and Grandpa can come out and we could go to a baseball game in Cincinnati?"

My eyes started watering as our brief conversation continued.

"Baseball in Cincinnati..."

"Yeah, Yankees will be in town for a three-game inter-league series in June. I could get tickets for Father's Day."

My eyes then started gushing by then as I was really choking up...

"Son... Son, I'd like that, and you know your Grandpa will *love* that."

"The Yankees are Grandpa's favorite team, and you know they're mine too. Listen Dad, I'm sorry for all the shit that happened with the way I mistreated Faith by what I wrote, and with what happened with Trystan's school, and I'm sorry for getting you thrown in jail."

"Son, it's all right. Thank you for saying that. We all know that I can be kind of a smart ass sometimes. I probably deserved some of it, but hey, it was great seeing DeShawn, Sedale and Danny again."

"DeShawn told me you made your free throws."

"I did. Tyler, I'm sorry for getting you all fired up before and after court."

"I'm sorry too, Dad."

"Good luck in Ohio."

Ten days later, I received a call from Faith.

"Dad, I just wanted to give you a heads up. I'm coming to Central Oregon for Easter weekend, and there's something you should know."

"What's that?"

"Our other grandpa is in St. Charles Hospital in Bend."

"Henry's in the hospital. Should I go see him?"

"Dad, we know that wouldn't be a good idea. The last time you were with him you almost got in a fight."

"Oh, that's right. Good point. I'm flying Down Under to Sydney on Friday for the Australian Ironman."

"That's good. But until Friday, be careful, will you, Dad? Mom's going to be in your neck of the woods and she's been freaking out lately because the I.R.S. man found her. She's now going to have to file bankruptcy since she hasn't paid her taxes since you two got divorced."

"Damn. Thanks for the heads up."

"Sure. Where are you staying, Dad, and how long will you be gone?"

"I'm there for three weeks. The first week before the triathlon, I'll be with Coach Barrie Suva in Sydney. After that, I'll be letting the spirit take me."

"Okay. Just please keep in touch. Dad, they don't think Grandpa is going to make it to the weekend. The lung cancer and the emphysema are winning the battle."

In the late afternoon of Easter Sunday, Faith e-mailed me some scanned documents. Her message confirmed the inevitable…

Dad,
Grandpa Henry died on Good Friday, just before midnight. He was 80 years old. Mom, Libby and Tyler were there, as were Uncle Daniel and Aunt Sherrie who were consoling Grandma Eileen.

From the land Down Under, I immediately called Faith.

"It was his time, Dad."

"How's your mom holding up?"

"Friday was hard on her but I think she's doing as well as we could expect."

"It's the end of an era. I'm sure he's feeling better now, wherever he may be."

"Yeah, Dad, and I think there was a silver lining to all of the tragedy."

"Silver lining?"

"Mom actually made peace with Grandpa Henry on Thursday. She told me that she and Daniel were sitting alone as Henry was sleeping while the others were getting lunch. All of a sudden, Grandpa sat up in his hospital bed and started crying and shouting, 'Diane Christine, where are you? I am so sorry, I've got to ask forgiveness for the terrible things I did to you when you were just a little girl, even when you were too young to remember.'"

"No way, Faith."

"Dad, it's true. Mom said he was sorry for doing bad things to her. Then Daniel joined in and said he saw their father doing things to her as well. Later, Daniel started in talking about the times he had molested her himself, and how he had recently asked Jesus for forgiveness, and he wanted her to forgive him as well."

"Wow. I didn't know if that day would ever come."

"And Dad, it gets even better. Grandma Eileen made us all Easter dinner and the kids hunted for eggs in the yard and right before we left, Mom gave me an Easter basket like she always does."

"That couldn't have been surprising."

"But this time in the basket she gave me something new. She gave me one of her journals."

"Does it smell like beer and cigs?"

"Dad, stop. I think we have a breakthrough, here.

"Was she hammered when she gave it to you?"

"Dad, I mean it. STOP. I've read the journal in its entirety and honestly, I think the message inside it was really meant for you."

"Huh?"

"Yes, I scanned the pages and they're attached to the e-mail I sent you."

"Thanks, Faith. Keep that journal with you in a safe place. Please don't lose it."

"Dad, there's one more thing I need to tell you before you read Mom's journal."

"Sure Faith. What is it?"

"Dad, I don't know exactly how to say this."

"Faith, just be straight with me. Spit it out. You know that's all I've ever asked of you."

"Dad, I owe you an apology. Last fall when things got really crazy, I was going through withdrawals from getting off the alcohol and I told Tyler and Libby that you had raped me. Dad, I'm sorry a million times. I thought I needed to say anything to get sympathy from anybody I could and I wanted to get my brother and sister back on my side. I know I threw you under the bus by doing this and I'm sure my actions didn't help your stalking case."

"It's okay, Faith. Sometimes when people don't tell the truth, when what they're saying is so bizarre, most people don't believe them anyway."

"I mean it this time, Dad. I AM sorry!"

"Thank you for coming clean, Faith. Let's take some time to ponder and we'll talk about this after I get back from Australia."

"I love you, Dad."

"I love you, Faith."

That night, I printed out the scanned pages and after pouring myself a cognac, I then took a seat on Barrie's back deck. Lighting a victory cigar in the cool Aussie evening, I opened Diane Christine Downer's journal.

Dear Jesus,

On this, the eve of your most sacred of all days, your resurrection, I want to send this message of thanks, love and praise.

My father here on Earth went to be with you yesterday, on Good Friday. Before he left, however, I feel he made his peace by lifting the darkest of dark clouds by saying he was sorry. Lord, I forgive him as I do forgive my brother, for asking forgiveness for his discretions against me as well.

In this same spirit, I'd like to offer my apologies lifted up to you so you may wash me of my sins.

Lord, forgive me.

Lord, please forgive me for the way I've wronged others. Whether or not it was a result of my faulty upbringing makes no difference. I'm the one who's responsible.

Lord, forgive me for the way I've mistreated my children throughout their lives. I ask forgiveness for not being the mother they deserve and for abusing them in ways throughout their lives as I was abused. I'm sorry for waking up with each of my three kids individually on more than one occasion, naked in their beds with them. I'm sorry for the things I did to my kids when they were young, things they can't remember, and maybe even more importantly, the things I can't even remember. Please help me to redeem myself in their eyes and to someday restore their trust in me.

I also ask forgiveness for all the times I demonstrated immoral sexuality toward their teenage friends and for the times throughout the years that I had intimate relations with the countless boys, especially Bobby Robbins, Salvino Perez, Zane Ketchner, and all of the others. I hope they've been able to live fruitful lives and work through the emotional scars I have inflicted upon them.

I'm also sorry for selling the drugs I took from Dr. Del Norte and the other doctors and for giving that Davron to Laura Hope. I'm sorry for not supervising those girls and renting that room at the Bard's Inn without supervising that party. My heart goes out to Laura Hope's parents. I can't even imagine what it would be like to lose a daughter, or a son, for that matter. That must be like living in hell on Earth. Please give them strength to carry on.

I'm sorry to Ashland Police Officer Vaughn Seward and even more to his wife, Michelle. What started out as a friendly meeting with Vaughn for a Star of David and dragon tattoo, turned into a one-night stand. Our indiscretions perpetuated my lies on the witness stand. I'm ashamed and remorseful.

I'm sorry for not being a better life partner. I'm sorry for not standing up for myself and letting Angie Crockford and Hannah pressure me to file the divorce papers. I'm sorry for hoarding the photo albums and tearing all of the pictures of Billy out of most of them. I promise I will give him the ones I have left so he can scan the remaining photos.

I'm sorry to you, Billy. I'm sorry I routinely laced your food with narcotics. I simply did not know how to respond to your high energy levels. I believe at one time we may have really loved each other, at least for a while when we were kids.

Billy, you are not a stalker.

You are a good man. You are a good dad and grandfather. You certainly haven't deserved all the mean-spirited destruction I've inflicted upon you for the past 30 years. I should have let you run free when you were 17.

I admit it. I have a problem, many problems. I'm sick. I need help. Please rid me of these addiction demons. Please help me.

I now lift up all these people before you, Lord. I pray that you'll resurrect their spirits so they may be healed as they grow to know, honor, and serve you.

In Jesus' holy name,

Amen.

~ Diane Christine Downer, April 23, 2011

The cigar and cognac tasted bittersweet, and I knew what had to be done. I forwarded the document to Elodie.

Two days later, as I was running the streets of Sydney, with music blasting through my iPhone, Elodie called. I stopped to answer.

"G'day, Elodie."

"G'day, Billy. I just finished a meeting with the D.A. and Diane's attorney Franklin Fortran. We looked over the documents you forwarded to me. Billy, do you have the original journal?"

"I don't. Faith has it."

"Could I drive by and get it from her?"

"Of course. I'll text you her address and phone number."

"Billy, this is huge for you. And things don't look good for Diane."

"What do you mean?"

"She indicts herself with this journal."

"I thought that might happen."

"Fortran just threw up his hands when he saw the pages. When we get the journal, I'm going to motion for a complete dismissal of any of the remaining charges. Fortran said he's going to advise her to halt going forward with the appeals process. Either way, chances are good that her "permanent LIFETIME" stalking protective order, as she called it, is not only going to be dismissed, but also immediately expunged from your record."

"Elodie, that *is* fantastic news. Now, what's going to happen to Downer?"

"It's highly likely that she'll be arrested. What they decide to charge her with is up to the D.A. but it could be the drugs, involvement in the Laura Hope tragedy, or a combination."

"What about her relationships with the teenage boys?"

"Well, that's a sticky one. The statute of limitations might have passed but we can't be so sure."

"Then how did the Catholic priests get nailed after all those years?"

"Interesting that you ask. That's why I called Bill Barton. He's one of my mentors."

"Is he the Bill Barton from Newport?"

"Yeah."

"I know him. He used to play in our three-on-three tournaments. He led his team, the Geriatric Stallions to the over-50, six-foot-and-under Global Championships in Barcelona. He's world famous."

"Yeah, I believe that. Bill is quite a character."

"Yeah, and I heard he put the Oregon Catholic Church into bankruptcy when he filed and won a class action suit by all of those former altar boys."

"It gets even more interesting, Billy. He's the first attorney who has ever been allowed to sue the Pope."

"Suing the Pope? No shit, Maddock?"

"Yeah."

"Damn, I ran into him at a Portland State men's basketball game a couple years ago and we met for a Spanish coffee after the game."

"At Huber's?"

"Yeah, the three of us will have to go there someday."

"Perfect."

"So what's really going to happen to Diane? What's your prediction? I want to be there for the kids."

"I can't make any promises, but she would be wise to go with a plea of 'guilty, due to insanity.' Either way, she'll be heading to Salem for a while, either to the state pen and/or the state mental hospital."

"Whew, I wish things didn't have to come to this."

"Billy, she will more than likely get out someday. You will need to be careful. The psychological studies show that women who find themselves in these situations have a high rate of someday stalking the person who they believe put them away."

"I will. Thanks for being here with me through all this."

"That's my job. Oh, and there was one more thing. I was hoping now that you will no longer be an official client of mine, maybe we could do Shakespeare again? Maybe something a little more light-hearted this time?"

"Sure, I say we do *Love's Labor's Lost*, this summer!"

"That sounds excellent, Billy, and good luck on your triathlon."

"Thanks, Elodie. I'd better get moving."

"Godspeed, Billy. You are the epitome of endurance."

Epilogue

Her name was Chantelle Douglas. I met her on a dating website on August 30th, 2001. She was the quintessential Aussie goddess—5'8", flowing blonde hair with blue eyes, ample breasts, long legs and a smile that would melt you faster than a sweaty Saharan sauna suit. She inspired me through numerous e-mail interactions and one brief, yet memorable phone exchange. She challenged me to *Test My Limits*, lifting me from the depression, destruction, and despair which a divorce of desperation so readily creates. She inspired me to dream of a journey Down Under, which I magically and meticulously arranged, only to see the trip aborted in April 2002 when my passport application was not renewed. Downer had reported to the State that I had not paid her child or spousal support, which was so wrong since it was so untrue. Therefore, my chance to meet Chantelle Douglas was denied.

Chantelle and I went our separate ways, losing contact until 2005. I tried reconnecting with her after I'd finished a number of triathlons, marathons and other endurance challenges. I sent her a short message of love and inquiry with some photos. Shortly thereafter, she reappeared with the following message:

Dear Billy,

How is my American sweetheart?

I just wanted to write to tell you I believe in you and I know you can do anything you put your mind to. I have and always will be so very proud of you. I think about you on a daily basis. I think of the connection we have together and I long for the day that we meet and I can look into your eyes and smile then kiss your sweet lips.

I dream some days about just sitting with you for hours and talking about our experiences, our visions, wants and desires, and then helping each other to fulfill those desires.

The way I look at things, babe, you are in my heart no matter how far we are apart. Every accomplishment I experience, I feel you here right beside me. I can see a place where our love never ends.

It is an honour being your friend, sweetheart, and as I am sitting here knowing I'd prefer to be spending my day running beside you.

And the pictures you sent are amazing! You look so incredible. When I first saw them, I became totally speechless and do you realize that in that picture with your sideburns and mustache you really do resemble Steve Prefontaine?

It amazes me how strong your connection is with him. It's like his spirit keeps drawing people into your life who revolve around him. I fully believe in my heart that each event you enter, each marathon you run and each triathlon you compete in, Pre is right there beside you. He's watching you, speaking to you, encouraging you, breathing rhythm into you, and pumping adrenaline through your veins.

I will never stop believing in his presence! Let me share an amazing story. Last September, I had to travel to Coogee Bay in Sydney to meet with a prospective investor in a business venture I am looking into.

Anyway, I was there in the late afternoon, when I put on my Nikes to go running in the grassy fields of Coogee's Dolphins Point. I had just passed the Bali Terrorist Bombing Memorial, the tall sculpture with the three interlocking "O's" which are symbolic for "family, friends and community," when I felt a warm, ocean breeze rush over me.

I was running well, feeling strong and free when right at about the three-kilometer mark, I stumbled and fell in the grass, and twisted my ankle.

As I rolled over in pain, I clutched my ankle with both hands. I clenched my teeth until the pain subsided and at that moment the clouds were forming overhead. I just lay back in the grass while looking at the clouds amidst the birth of another sunset. The sky was a combination of brilliant colors: purple, pink, silver and blue.

And as I stared at the moving clouds, they stopped for a brief moment and I swear to this day the face of Steve Prefontaine appeared in the clouds for an instant, and then that face turned into you, Billy Freeman, and then back into Pre. Everything at that moment became silent. I heard no traffic, no birds, and no waves crashing nearby on the shore. I heard nothing but complete silence and I was mesmerized with the faces I was seeing in the clouds looking down upon me.

It was like Pre was trying to tell me something but I couldn't be sure exactly what. I know I wanted to reach out and touch him, to see if I had a hold of reality.

Then, in the amount of time it took for the images to appear, the faces vanished. I heard a noise over to my right. There was a man approaching and he started speaking. Since my concentration had been broken, I sat up. The kind man asked me if I was okay since he had seen me fall from almost a kilometer away.

I politely told him I was fine. He didn't seem convinced. In fact he said that I seemed "dazed."

I told him I wasn't awestruck because of the fall, but because of what I'd just witnessed in the clouds. Then, I lay on my back in the grass trying to see Pre's face again, but the clouds had shifted and the image never returned.

Anyway, that night I had my business meeting. I know I'm rambling and by now you probably think I'm crazy for thinking this, but a greater power was edging me on to run after my next dream...

Someday soon, I'll be opening a triathlon store featuring Nike shoes and Pre-themed running attire. It'll be located in Coogee Bay, inside Titan Fitness near Dolphins Point.

Anyway that night back in my hotel room I was exhausted and my ankle was swollen so I decided to make it an early night. I fell asleep right away, but in the early morning hours something woke me. I felt a presence in the room; it was strong and when I looked over at the glowing clock, it said 3:03 a.m. I turned on the lamp beside my bed and nobody and nothing were there but I was sure I felt something in that room with me.

I hope you'll come and run with me someday and see my new triathlon store called *Chantelle's Endurance Shop*.

Keep moving,

Love always,

Chantelle

After receiving a message like that, one would be crazy not to drop everything and get to Coogee Bay! I had Googled to find her triathlon shop near Sydney but to no avail. Since originally Chan had been living in Brisbane, which is where she claimed to be, I started focusing my search efforts there. So in 2008 I had gotten my passport returned and thus journeyed to Brisbane and the Gold Coast. I ran all throughout the city of Brisbane and the Gold Coast over the course of two short weeks; I contacted the authorities, the newspapers and even posted lost-person flyers seeking Chantelle. Sadly, my efforts did not produce her.

Then in 2010, Chantelle, my Aussie zephyr, returned. This time she called me leaving a message of four words... *IronMan Australia, Port Macquarie.*

In the ten years since the divorce, I'd run sixteen marathons, finished three Ironman triathlons, and was about to finish my fourth in Port Macquarie. The day was beautiful. The swim was amazing in the Hastings River, which flows into the Pacific. We started and finished near the Town Wharf Marina. The bike leg took off from there, venturing out and back south of Port Macquarie on Pacific Drive, a simply breathtaking ride with a view of the ocean for the majority of the course. On the return ride into Port Mac, I was mesmerized and after passing a mate on my right, I asked him while cruising at about forty-four kilometers per hour, amidst the sunshine, blue sky and the breakers in complete view: "Mate, is this heaven?"

"I don't see any angels, mate," he replied, "but it is a great place to be."

"It *IS* a great place to be, and I think I *AM* seeing angels!"

The marathon portion of the course was a unique, four-lap challenge on a relatively flat layout. My total time was a personal record at 10:30.03. I know I should have been thrilled when I learned I had finally qualified for a trip to the World Championships in October in Kona. However, I knew that for the last ten years my own personal endurance event had been simply to meet Chantelle Douglas. I had just wanted to see her, and make sure she was alive and safe. I wanted to give her a hug, thank her for her positive impact on me and my life, and express my pure gratitude for simply keeping me going.

So I journeyed back to Sydney immediately after the event and rested up for a few hours at the home of my basketball coaching exchange friend, the legendary Barrie "Suve" Suva.

"How you going today, mate?" asked Suve.

"How am I going? I'm going to try to run a few kilometers."

"The soreness has subsided?"

"Most of it. Yeah, I feel amazing. I think it's because I'm taking this new product called RegeniCare from Univera. It's totally natural, plant-based and backed by scientific research, double-blind placebo studies."

"Where are you off to?"

"Dolphins Point in Coogee Bay."

"Dang, if I weren't coaching at the local Catholic school today, I'd take you down there myself."

"That's okay, Suve, I don't think I'll be alone."

"If you wait until tomorrow I can take you."

"That's all right, mate. I feel the need to go today."

"Be sure to stop at the pub at the Hotel Coogee Bay, it's just across the beach on Arden Street."

"Will do."

"Say hello to my buddy, Paul at the bar. His nickname is Snake. Be sure to tell Snake the mantra when it comes to beer, 'Mates can never say nay to the Coogee Bay!'"

"Perfect, Suve. I'll have the cab driver take me there, and Barrie, what do you know about why it's called 'Dolphins Point,' anyway?"

"It's called Dolphins Point because in 2003 the town council voted to honor six Coogee Bay Dolphins rugby players and many other Aussies killed in the Bali terrorist attack. It's a place of remembrance and reflection for the community, and for all the families, friends and teammates affected by the tragedy."

On the drive toward Coogee, I struck up a conversation with the taxi driver. His name was Sayid Ahktar. He was from Pakistan. He had dark skin, dark eyes, and dark hair which appeared naturally curly. He had a traditional Pakistani beard. His English was amazing. I asked him if he had seen the popular American-made television show, *LOST* as I pointed out that he looked exactly like Sayid Jarrah, the Iraqi Republican Guard veteran from the show.

"*LOST*? Of course, my favorite character is Dr. Jack Shephard and we all know that Oceanic Flight 815 departed from Sydney. We used to have people come over to my house every week to watch. Many people have told me that I remind them of Sayid from the show. I'm not Iraqi and I don't know about your beliefs, but I'm Pakistani Shiite Muslim. We don't believe in suicide bombings or car bombings. The Sunni Muslims are the ones tied in with Taliban. I hate Osama bin Laden."

"Why is that?"

"Bin Laden is mother fucker."

"I know a lot of people who feel the same way as you do, Sayid, including myself. Now, why do you say that?"

"Bin Laden and Taliban killed my father."

"No shit, Sayid?"

I couldn't believe what I was hearing.

"Yes."

"How come?"

"My father was a cleric, and his beliefs did not match that of Taliban."

"Just because they didn't agree on their views?"

"Yes, and bin Laden and Taliban were stalking my father for months, maybe even years, before gunning him down."

"So is this why you're in Australia?"

"Yes. I'm a refugee. They would have killed me also if I would have stayed."

"How old were you when you left, Sayid?"

"Nineteen. I was in first year of college when Taliban brought down World Trade Towers."

I noticed us driving onto Malabar Road. I smiled as I pondered my favorite D.H. Lawrence short story, "The Rocking Horse Winner," about the boy who wanted to get luck, and then money, so he could win the affection and love of his inattentive mother. Shortly thereafter, Malabar Road turned into Arden Street. I could see the Pacific clearly to my right. It was bluer than in the ending of *The Shawshank Redemption*...I became hypnotized.

"There's Coogee Bay," said Sayid. "And here's the Coogee Bay Hotel, just up on our left."

"Where's Dolphins Point?"

Sayid pointed to hill to the right.

"It's up there in the grassy area beyond those rocks to the right of those eucalyptus trees. That's Dunningham Park."

Sayid stopped the car. I handed him some cash and then started to get out of the car. "Sayid, where's the memorial for the victims of the terrorist bombing?"

Before Sayid could answer, I saw the sculpture. It was one from a picture Chantelle had sent me. I wanted to say goodbye to Sayid, make a dash to the sculpture, but just then my iPhone vibrated...It was an Associated Press news FLASH...

"JESUS, Sayid! You aren't going to believe this...I showed him the iPhone...the BREAKING NEWS FLASH...

"OSAMA BIN LADEN IS DEAD!"

"YES, Praise be to Allah!" shouted Sayid. "President Obama must have got that mother fucker."

"Actually, the story seems to say that it was the Navy Seals."

"Who cares? This is wonderful!"

"DAMN, Sayid! What are the chances? Park the cab! Let's go have a drink and celebrate! Never say nay, to the Coogee Bay!"

The people in the pub at the Coogee Bay Hotel went ballistic! We ordered at least six schooners of Carlton Draught and many of the mates there were in tears watching the television coverage.

One thing I've discovered in Australia is that you can get hammered and still work out. You can get hammered and still play basketball. You can get hammered and still go running. So after Sayid and I exchanged contact info, that's exactly what I did. I went running.

I wore the same attire Elodie had given me back in the States. I threw on my headphones and blasted Enigma's *The Platinum Collection* inside my mind from the iPhone. As I started running around the perimeter of the bay, I smiled as I could still see the memorial sculpture in the distance. Instead of running directly toward it first, I felt drawn down Arden Street and then left on Alfreda Street just another block to the east. There it was…Titan Fitness.

It didn't take long for me to see the signs:."Chantelle's Endurance Shop" and "Grand Opening."

I floated through the main entrance seeking the Aussie angel. The place was buzzing. It looked like she had it all: Cervelo Bikes, Zipp and Rolf wheels, a myriad of styles and brands of wetsuits, and Nike shoes and attire to go along with a wide array of training and competition accessories. I noticed three incredible framed images on the walls above. The first was a movie poster from *Fire on the Track: The Steve Prefontaine Story*. Next was a 36-inch square enlarged image from the Journey *E5C4P3* album. Third was another picture of Pre; this one was the world-renowned and hard-to-find Nike Godspeed print, depicting three images of Pre amidst a Hayward Field backdrop.

A crowd was gathered in the store as Aussies Miranda "Rinnie" Carfrae and Chris "Macca" McCormack were signing posters commemorating their IronMan World Championship crowns which they had earned in Kona last October. Also in attendance were Aussie greats Pete Jacobs (yesterday's winner at Port Mac), Craig Alexander (former world champ who sat out of Port Mac because of illness), and Swiss beauty Caroline Steffan, yesterday's women's winner at Port Mac.

Everybody was going nuts over the end of Bin Laden!

Macca actually stood and approached me.

"Macca! Weren't you in Alaska last summer?"

"Yeah, Billy! I remember you. We met at Beaker's! Have you heard from Rebecca?"

Macca was referring to my dear friend, Rebecca "Beaker" McKee, who is the top triathlon training coach in Alaska. She even has her own training facility, called PEAK Centre for Human Performance. She trains people from all over the world.

"Beaker's going a million miles an hour, like always. Triathlon is really becoming the rage in Anchorage and if anybody wants to become a triathlete, or become the best triathlete they can be, then Rebecca is the one who can whip their butt into shape."

"Billy, have you met Chantelle yet?"

"Well, not exactly, I guess."

"She's around here somewhere. I bet the two of you would hit it off. Now, I'm off for a quick ride."

"See you later, Macca."

"See you later. Oh, look over there, coming out from the back, there she is."

Yes.

There she was.

For a moment, time seemed to freeze. No matter how much I'd rehearsed this moment, I couldn't predict the effect it would have on me. To come to the end of a long journey and to meet someone who you've wanted to meet, the mind can't control the body any more than the body can control the mind.

I admit that I was a bit embarrassed, but I was stunned. I couldn't move. I was finally about to meet the person who had driven me for almost a decade.

Before I could react to my surroundings, she made eye contact with me and for another moment, time stood still. When I snapped out of it, we approached each other.

She reached out her hands and I took both of them in mine. We then exchanged a warm, lengthy embrace, followed by a wonderful kiss.

"Billy! I knew you'd show up someday!"

"Chan, I was just out running and just happened to be in the area."

"Just happened to be in the area? I saw that you qualified for Kona!"

"Chan, were you at Port Mac?"

"Yeah, I came in about thirty minutes behind you."

"No kidding, Wow! I'm surprised we didn't see other in the recovery tent."

"I looked for you on the massage tables and at the post-race food area. But I had to get back to the store. I have a bit of time now. Shall we run?"

"I was hoping you'd ask."

"Let me go tell my store manager that I'm heading out and I'll be back after a while."

"That's great, Chan, and your store is beautiful. It is exactly how I envisioned it."

"It's exactly how *WE* envisioned it, Billy."

So Chantelle Douglas and I *finally* got to run together for REAL.

She took me all around Dolphins Point, near the coastline, and returning to the Park Memorial. We rolled around in the grass, hugging and laughing for a few moments. We stared up at the sky while also staring at the Bali Memorial Sculpture.

"Chan, didn't you once tell me the sculpture figures represent *family, friends* and *community*."

"Exactly, Billy. Besides health and faith, family, friends and community are the most important elements for living a fruitful life."

"I couldn't agree with you more."

"The sculpture also represents the Aussie spirit of courage and endurance."

"That's breathtaking."

"The figures also symbolize life, growth, hope, and strength in unity. Individually, each figure could be easily toppled, but joined together they form a strong and supported whole structure."

We held hands and stared into the Pacific and the deep blue Australian sky. I was brought out of my trance by my phone ringing.

"I'm sorry, Chantelle."

"Take the call, Billy."

It was my buddy, Chris "Flash" Gordon, calling from the States. I put the phone on speaker.

"Flash! What's going on?"

"I watched you finish your Ironman triathlon on the Internet. You were smoking that victory cigar as you crossed the finish. That was too cool. When you get back, I want you to teach me how to become an Ironman."

"Of course, Flash! And someday you'll light your own victory cigar. It's a tradition."

"Awesome! And Billy, I've got great news. You know Brent Barker, my business partner who's involved with numerous film projects. Brent's company, Strata Capital Group, has negotiated and agreed upon terms with a major movie company to turn your novel, *Goddess Seeker,* into a major motion picture. They've got an award-winning screenwriter who'll convert your story into a script and get this…they've even lined up the actor to play your main character, Steven Jenny. All they need is your blessing."

"Flash, you know I trust you. If you endorse this deal then I'm all in."

"Who's the actor for the lead role?"

"Well, the competition was fierce! The finalists included Johnny Depp, Tom Cruise, and others. It was a tough call, but the person who's been chosen to play Steven Jenny is…

Matthew Fox."

I saw Chantelle's eyes light up with the announcement.

"He's that doctor from *LOST*," said Flash.

"That's great. I think he just might be perfect."

"Mr. Fox is looking forward to meeting you, Billy. He's a big fan of yours."

"Flash, the feeling's mutual. I gotta run, so talk to you later."

Chantelle could hardly contain herself. When I ended the conversation with Flash, she dived into me with a ferocity that would make Oregon football coach Chip Kelly proud.

"A movie, Billy! Your story is going to be on the silver screen!"

"Pretty cool, huh, Chantelle?"

"I'd say so. I think a celebration is in order."

"I agree, Chan, but I say let's do it Oregon."

"Why not here?"

"Baby, I don't want to rain on your parade. It's your grand opening. And everyone's going to be going crazy for at least a week with the bin Laden news. You need to work your business. There will always be time for us later."

"Don't you want to make love, Billy? I always thought that was our destiny."

"Oh, you know I do. But I want you to get your business rolling and then come to my world. Besides, there's someone I want you to meet."

"Okay, Billy. I can come at the end of July."

"Wonderful, Chantelle. I'll see you then."

We embraced for one final time and exchanged another warm, friendly kiss.

She made a dash back to her store.

I watched...then I ran into the sunset.